A Dangerous Time for Dogs

The Long Journey Home

Eric Armstrong

First paperback edition 24\09\21

Book design by Publishing Push
Cover Illustrations by Natalie Stead

ISBNs:
Paperback: 978-1-80227-212-3
eBook: 978-1-80227-213-0

To my parents, Eric and Vera, in recognition of their love and encouragement.

Acknowledgements

I have to start by talking about Trevor, a remarkable Patterdale terrier, who was my inspiration for writing this book. He had a love of life and a sense of fun that endeared him to people. Sadly, Trevor was involved in a road traffic accident some years ago and did not survive. He is remembered by all who knew him.

Poppy, the Lhasa apso of the story, is part of the family and something of a prima donna. I started writing short stories about her many adventures three years ago that I published online and which inevitably led me to write this novel.

I must also thank my wife, Pam, for her support and patience during the last three years when she was forced to spend many afternoons alone as I battled with the text. I also read the whole book to her on a number of occasions. Well done, Pam.

Thanks to my son James, who persuaded me to write the novel in the first place, and my elder brother Terry, who spent long hours on the telephone with me, talking about the merits of good grammar whilst we edited the text.

Finally, an apology and a thank you to my taxi colleagues and customers, whom I constantly talked to about the book. Thanks to you all.

Contents

Chapter One

In the Beginning

The storm gathered strength as huge raindrops, driven horizontally by the gale-force wind, battered the stone walls of the old house. The torrential rain was accompanied by flashes of lightning, and deafening claps of thunder concentrated directly overhead. In the noise and confusion created by the squall, two puppies burst through a badly damaged barn door that had been all but blown off its hinges. Other dogs remained, cowering within the structure, terrified by the fury of the storm raging outside. Undeterred and desperate to escape, the two young animals made for a wooden gate that was swinging violently back and forth. As the pair approached this dangerously unstable barrier, it slammed shut, almost in their faces, and they both veered off in another direction. Moving on at speed, they searched for a gap in the fence that would afford them an exit to the fields beyond the compound. Suddenly, Milo, the leading dog, lurched to the right and sped through a gaping hole, followed closely by his injured friend.

Both puppies had jet black fur, which happened to be the only similarity between the two. Dima, the second escapee, was much bigger than his companion and three times as strong, even though the pair were more or less the same age. Milo, the smaller dog, had lived and suffered with Dima and the other dogs in the most appalling conditions for almost twelve months. Together, the pair had formed an unbreakable bond, always promising each other that they would stay together forever, regardless of the circumstances. Once clear of the fence, they hurtled across the fields, slipping in and out of the shadows, making identification difficult for any would-be pursuers. At this stage, however, there were none.

Earlier in the day, Dima had been provoked into attacking one of the thugs supposedly responsible for his care and wellbeing. This action, although not without justification, had earned the young puppy a vicious and sustained beating. His subsequent injuries were severe and painful and considerably hindered his progress across the wet grass. Milo was very concerned for his friend and allowed him all the time he needed to reach the trees on the far side of the field. He remained calm and in control, employing all his senses to seek a path away from their wretched place of confinement. Now travelling more slowly, it took a while to reach cover but, eventually, the forest enveloped them both and provided a safe haven, at least for the time being. Relieved but exhausted, Milo sniffed the air, breathing in the sweet scent of freedom.

The storm had arrived unexpectedly and was unusually destructive. As a result, it required an urgent response from the three men tasked with the security of the site and all the buildings within the property's perimeter. Although it was already dark, these men acted very quickly, yelling instructions to each other and doing such repairs as were necessary to secure the barn and the wooden gate beyond. At first, they had no idea that two dogs had escaped and just busied themselves with their work. It wasn't long, however, before they realised that a pair of disruptive puppies were missing.

Two of the men became very agitated by this sudden disappearance and wanted to organise a search immediately, fearing serious repercussions from their employer. Nevertheless, the man in charge decided to delay the pursuit until early the following morning. He felt confident that two young dogs with absolutely no experience of the outside world would not get very far at night, particularly in the middle of a terrifying storm. In addition, he knew only too well that one of the dogs was carrying a debilitating injury.

Quietly standing within the comparative safety of the forest, the two fugitives considered their options, which appeared to be extremely limited. Milo was intelligent and already aware of the dangers of staying too long in one place. His injured friend, on the other hand, desperately needed to rest. Reluctantly, he resolved to seek out a secure hiding place where they could wait out the storm and then prepare for the inevitable pursuit. Although Milo knew for certain that the humans would come, running was no longer a viable option. After discussing the situation with his friend, it was agreed that both dogs should concentrate on finding a place of safety.

The teeming rain had flooded the earth, creating a treacherous surface that severely hampered their progress through the forest. Nonetheless, the two companions finally arrived at a place deemed suitable by the smaller puppy.

Here, the trees and thick undergrowth afforded them both numerous places capable of concealment. Each dog chose a safe hiding place and then settled down to wait, confident that they had until morning to rest and then prepare themselves for what may lie ahead.

Early the following day, in slightly more favourable weather, the search for the missing dogs began. The foreman determined that the nearby forest would be the most obvious place to start looking, and so three men and an experienced tracking dog set off in that direction. The leader calculated that the pair were likely to remain together, which would dramatically reduce their chances of escape. In normal circumstances, and considering the waterlogged terrain, the hunters would have expected a couple of healthy animals to give their trackers a good run for their money. On this occasion, however, they knew that one of the puppies was badly injured and would struggle to cover the ground quickly. Every now and then, they found paw prints in the still sodden earth, boosting their confidence that both dogs would be caught very quickly. They were only partially right, however, because, in less than an hour, the men had located the first hiding place and secured the larger dog. Dima had been easy to find but far more difficult to restrain and, given his injuries, did well to resist their attempts to bring him under control. It took longer than it should have but, finally, Dima just dropped to the ground and was recaptured. He was completely exhausted. The pursuers were jubilant and felt certain that the remaining puppy would also be recaptured without further delay.

After resuming the search, however, the team discovered paw prints all around the undergrowth — hundreds of them going in every direction. Even the dog was confused and unable to pick up a scent. The men already knew that the missing puppy was very capable and perhaps cunning enough to stay one step ahead of them. Despite their misgivings, they were unwilling to concede defeat and continued their fruitless efforts for hours until it finally dawned on them that they had been outwitted. They began to realise that their very capable quarry could well be miles away. Rather than admit to their boss that they had been hoodwinked by a puppy, they decided to tell him that Milo had drowned in the storm. The men knew that repercussions might follow the loss of this dog but hoped that their cover story would protect them to some extent.

After the hunters had left the area and silence returned to the forest, a small black dog, covered in thick grey mud, slowly emerged from a deep puddle close to the bushes that had concealed his companion. Milo looked around and realised he was completely alone for the first time in his short life. Although free, he was desperately unhappy because his liberty had come at a terrible cost. Dima, his closest friend, had been recaptured by these criminal humans, and it was entirely Milo's fault. The solemn pledge that the two of them would always stay together had been broken. As Dima was forcibly dragged away, the last words that his friend had called out he would never forget.

"Milo, my friend, what have you done?"

Chapter Two

Five Years Later

Heavy rock music combined with the high pitched whine of a vehicle driven at full throttle must have been audible for miles around as a shabby white transit van thundered along country lanes at an alarming and dangerous speed. On this early autumn morning, clear blue skies and stunning views created an image that encapsulated the beauty of the landscape. Unfortunately, the enchanting sounds of the countryside were completely drowned out by the irritating noise of the van. As the driver approached one of the small villages on their route, those locals already up and about recoiled in horror at the strident sound of the vehicle's engine as it accelerated along the High Street. The peace and tranquillity of the village were shattered as the van raced past the neighbourhood paper shop, narrowly missed two traffic bollards, and then continued erratically on its way. From beginning to end, the whole episode had probably taken less than sixty seconds. In the front of the van, the driver was enjoying himself immensely and laughing contemptuously at his older companion, who was desperately but ineffectively trying to slow him down.

Prior to leaving their base, the two men had been given instructions that were, as usual, clearly defined and unambiguous. Their employer had stressed that, wherever possible, they were to avoid any major roads and keep predominantly to the country lanes and back doubles. More importantly, they had been told to drive in such a way that would not attract unwanted attention, particularly from the local police.

Unfortunately, Dave Dixon, the musclebound thug at the wheel, was almost totally out of control and, much to the consternation of his more rational companion, could not be persuaded to follow orders and drive in the manner laid down by their boss. No matter how much Bernie French, his partner in crime, tried to persuade him to think about the consequences of his irresponsible behaviour, Dave merely ignored him. Luckily, however, the deteriorating road surfaces on the increasingly narrow lanes eventually forced him to slow down and drive in a rather more responsible manner.

Sadly, this more prudent approach was short-lived because, immediately after passing a road sign almost completely obscured by foliage, Dave cursed loudly and quickly brought the car to a sudden, juddering halt. Bernie, who was completely unprepared for this reckless manoeuvre, was propelled forward, almost smacking his head on the dashboard.

14

"What the hell was that all about, Dave?" Bernie was furious now and turned on his friend. "What are you trying to do? Kill us both?"

"Put a sock in it, mate," Dave responded sarcastically. "I missed the turning, that's all. Use the seatbelt next time, you mug."

Whilst this brief altercation was taking place, Dave reversed back about fifty yards and then turned sharp left onto an uneven track bordered on each side by tall trees and hedgerows. The metalled road surface was badly potholed, forcing Dave to move forward cautiously. Both men were now alert and extremely tense as the vehicle edged closer to a solitary cottage about two hundred yards ahead of them.

"Keep it slow, Dave."

"That's the place, Bernie!" The driver pointed to the cottage enthusiastically.

The older man was more cautious. "Hold on a second, Dave; there's a motor on the drive. This guy was supposed to be out. Turn around, mate. Let's get out of here!"

The younger man was deep in thought. "Don't panic, Bernie. Let's check it out first."

As the two villains watched, a small dog emerged from the far side of the cottage and settled in the front garden just inside the wooden gate, some fifty yards away.

"Well, stone me, Bernie." Dave whistled through his teeth. "This is our lucky day, son. I'll spin the van round while you have a shufti. Then I'll snatch the dog. We can be in and out in a few seconds."

The big man was very confident now and moved the vehicle along the uneven surface, taking great care to keep the engine noise to an absolute minimum. As the car moved ominously forward, these mean spirited felons prepared to snatch a small, defenceless dog.

Minutes before the transit had entered the lane, Poppy, a three-year-old Lhasa apso, had been enjoying the early October sunshine, sprawled out in her dad's vegetable patch, lazily chewing sticks and keeping one eye open for mischief. This small dog was a perfect example of her breed, predominantly white in colour with black fur covering the lower part of her face and the tips of her ears.

Gentle in nature but very intelligent, she had lived with her human family since birth. The little dog watched as her dad emerged from the cottage and strode energetically down the path. The house had a long garden, complete with an expansive lawn enclosed by trees and bushes. Towards the rear of the garden, there was a rubbish heap next to a large wooden shed. Poppy's dad entered the shed and reappeared a few moments later with the machine that cuts the grass.

This was never a happy event for the small dog, particularly when the mower was headed in her direction. While Poppy loved her human parents and the wonderful life they provided, she hated this machine with a passion and avoided it whenever possible. It was very noisy, irritatingly dusty and more than a little bit frightening. Needless to say, she chose not to remain in this environment longer than was necessary and retreated along the path that snaked around the side of the house and into the front garden. It was far better in this new location. Although Poppy could still hear the relentless whirring of the mower in the background, the front garden was relatively peaceful. She then headed for her favourite spot, the flower bed just inside the front gate, where she hoped to continue her afternoon activities.

Peace at last, or so she thought. As the young Lhasa settled down on the grass, something startled her. Poppy raised her head, sniffed the air and looked around. Dogs have exceptional abilities and can sense when something is not quite right. This was one of those occasions. Her late morning relaxation had not only been broken by the sound of the lawnmower but also by a second noise that she could not identify. She moved closer to the gate but, being a relatively small dog, couldn't see anything beyond the fence. Ominously, however, about fifty yards away, a worn-out transit van was slowly approaching the house. Although the

17

penetrating sound of the mower persisted, it was no longer the most significant issue.

Dogs tune in to the sights, sounds and smells of their surroundings, and all Poppy's senses screamed danger. She edged away from the gate but remained on high alert, believing that something dreadful was about to happen. Just then, she watched as a large vehicle drove slowly up to the front gate and stopped directly outside. A man, moving furtively, slipped into the garden, enabling Poppy to study him carefully. He was small and skinny with grey hair and a sallow complexion.

Poppy shuddered when she caught sight of the cold-blooded expression on his face as he surveyed his surroundings. He seemed to ignore the dog completely while he walked stealthily down the path leading to the back garden. Poppy's eyes stayed riveted on the intruder so intently that she failed to notice that the van outside the gate had been turned around. Had she been more alert, she could have taken evasive action, but it was far too late now. As she concentrated her attention on the first man, a second man leapt from the van and, in one sudden movement, grabbed her collar.

After making sure he had secured her, the second stranger jabbed something sharp into her hind leg, lifted her up, returned to the van and tossed her unceremoniously into the back. Poppy hit the floor very hard and rolled over. Her head ached from the impact, and her senses were fading, but she did detect the stale scent of animals and realised, with a rising feeling of dread, that other dogs had spent time there. The last thing she heard, before the doors slammed shut, was heavy, laboured breathing as the older man hurried back up the path. In no time at all, the van started moving again, now at a much faster pace than before.

The whole operation had taken mere seconds and Poppy's dad, still mowing the lawn in the back garden, remained blissfully unaware of her kidnap. In the front of the van, the two villains were jubilant, all traces of their recent bickering forgotten in the success of the moment.

"That was really easy, mate." said the bigger man. "One Lhasa apso in the can, Bernie." He smiled to himself, grunted and laughed. "The old man has got to be pleased with that! What little doggie is next on the list?"

Bernie was laughing too. "Maybe later. Let's find a pub, mate, cos I fancy a sherbet" He looked at his companion and grinned. "There'll be nothing for you, though, driver. I know what you're like when you've had a drink."

Even Dave had to laugh at that.

Alone and frightened, Poppy was very drowsy and not at all well. In less than a few minutes, she had been snatched from her garden, bundled into the back of a van and driven away. She was smart enough to know the trouble she was in, but the drug injected into her aching leg was taking hold and making it difficult for her to stay conscious. The reality of her predicament was now dawning on her — she was on her own, without family and without support. Much later, she would reflect on the events of that afternoon, particularly recalling how very easily evil had entered her world. At that point, everything changed. The life she had known in the past, and the happiness that underpinned it, seemed lost to her, perhaps forever. The last thing Poppy heard before sleep overwhelmed her was the sound of human laughter. Meanwhile, the van rumbled relentlessly on.

Chapter Three

Kidnap and Captivity

During the last few months, Bernie French had considered himself blessed for a few very good reasons. Following his recent release from prison, he had managed to secure steady employment, a reasonably good income and even accommodation. The fact that the job was illegal didn't really bother him very much. Bernie was a recidivist and, as a result, had spent at least fifteen years of his adult life in prison. He didn't touch spirits but had a weakness for beer. He was also a chain smoker, and the effects of nicotine had wreaked havoc on both his face and lungs as well as browned his teeth and left him with a hacking cough. He wore his forty-five years badly, being somewhat gaunt with a lined face that bore an unhealthy pallor. The man looked and sounded considerably older than his years.

Bernie worked for Charles Grey and his wife Joan, who ran a dog rescue business in the sticks — although almost all of the dogs were not so much rescued as stolen. When asked to recruit another person of similar background to himself, he immediately thought of his old cellmate, Dave Dixon, a vicious twenty-six-year-old villain with a quick temper and a capacity for violence. He had been approaching the end of a five-year sentence for burglary and assault and was due to leave prison a few days after Bernie. Dave was a big man, well above six feet tall, with a heavily muscled frame. Both his arms were adorned with rather garish tattoos and, engraved into the skin across the back of his neck, were the words "You're Next." This man was a force to be reckoned with and clearly not a person to cross.

In spite of their diverse personalities, the two men had become close friends. Bernie had assumed the role of a father figure to the younger man and, during their time in prison, had managed to keep him out of trouble on more than one occasion. Similarly, Dave had frequently looked after his best mate when Bernie had behaved unwisely and said the wrong things to the wrong people. Surprisingly, despite the age difference, they got on really well together and enjoyed doing what the Greys paid them to do, which, apart from a bit of maintenance work at the rescue centre, was stealing dogs to order. Basically, both men were more than willing to help their new bosses in whatever way they deemed necessary.

On this particular occasion, the two ex-cons had left base very early on an unusually bright October morning and had managed to snatch two dogs by early afternoon. In Dave's opinion, it was a very successful outcome and certainly sufficient for one day. Bernie, on the other hand, took an entirely different view. The whole enterprise had not been as easy as they had hoped because the second dog had been a significant challenge. Neither man had anticipated that the dog in question would have sunk its teeth into Bernie's hand, causing him to panic and administer an excessive amount of tranquiliser. By any standards, this dose would not be considered safe, and Bernie was just beginning to comprehend what the result of his rashness might be. The animal had not yet regained consciousness and appeared to be in a very poor condition. This turn of events could prove to be disastrous for Bernie, especially working for criminals. Getting fired could be the least of his problems.

Inside the van, Dave glanced over at his friend, who was sweating profusely and seemed to be scared.

Bernie spoke in a strained whisper. "It's an overdose, Dave, I swear. I was stupid angry and gave the mutt too much."

"Don't be a mug, Bernie. That thing attacked us both. Just look at the state of your hand, mate — so don't you worry. After we stop for another drink, we'll take our time and, with any luck, the boss will be tucked up in bed by the time we get home. It'll be fine. That vicious mongrel will probably be running about by morning."

Bernie glanced down at his right hand, tightly bound up with a bloody handkerchief. "You'd better be right, Dave, or Grey will have my guts."

Despite his legitimate concerns, Bernie's spirits were lifted by Dave's no-nonsense assessment of the situation and his suggestion that they take their time on the journey back to base. The boss might complain about their actions, but rather a tongue lashing for being late than turning up with a comatose dog. Dave, in accordance with his new timetable, slowed down to look for a suitable pub in which to grab a bite to eat. Much to Bernie's irritation, the big man passed a few acceptable places along the way but eventually pulled into a car park that lay behind a rather seedy-looking pub.

As is common with those involved in criminal activities, both men studied their immediate environment meticulously before getting out of the van. As Dave swaggered into the pub, Bernie warned him not to drink too much. Experience had taught him that alcohol made his friend extremely aggressive, and when in one of those moods, he was capable of causing a lot of trouble. To put it simply, Dave enjoyed hurting people.

Whilst the two men had been busy discussing the ramifications of Bernie's actions, Poppy, the traumatised Lhasa apso, had woken up suddenly feeling nauseous and with an awful taste in her mouth. The atmosphere in the van was stuffy, and the floor was running wet because the water bowl, previously full and within her reach, was now upside down on the floor and inaccessible. In addition, the van was no longer moving, and there was no indication of a human presence in her immediate vicinity. This fact should have reassured the small dog, but it rather served to heighten her feelings of apprehension.

As Poppy stretched out her body and looked around, she could just make out the shape of an enormous animal slumped on the floor only feet away from where she lay. The reality of her plight frightened her more than at any time since the kidnap because, whatever this creature was, it could well present a serious threat. Poppy settled down and listened to its laboured breathing interspersed with the whining normally associated with an animal in distress. To be sharing this cramped space with a comatose but potentially savage predator terrified her.

The most daunting aspect of the whole situation was the possibility that her companion could wake up at any time and attack her. If this were to happen, she would be alone and defenceless without a single soul to help her. She peered into the darkness hoping for answers but found none. As far as the little dog could recollect, she had been alone in the van immediately following her kidnap, but events after that were shrouded in a fog of uncertainty. Poppy concluded that the humans had captured this monster while she had been asleep. As a result, she became ever more fretful, chained up so alarmingly close to a dangerous creature and with no apparent means of escape. Her life could be in danger and, to negotiate the situation successfully, a cool head would be required. There were no easy choices here, so, in an attempt to further her knowledge, the young dog shuffled forward as far as the chain would allow. She stared into the darkness and growled fiercely in the hope that this might frighten the beast a little.

Although small, the Lhasa apso is known as the little lion dog because, when one of these impressive animals looks in the mirror, they see the reflection of a mighty lion. Poppy growled again but, after receiving no response, she retreated as far as the chain would allow and sank to the floor in despair. The huge animal groaned again and rolled over. At that precise moment, the tension was broken by the clearly audible sound of footsteps on the gravel, followed by the van doors opening and closing. Then Poppy heard the sound of laughter coming through a small grill between the two compartments. The two felons had returned, and almost immediately, the vehicle started moving again.

Feeling much better, Bernie was studying the map whilst simultaneously barking out instructions to the man Charles Grey had placed in charge of this enterprise. A sudden right turn caused the van to rock violently before the driver regained control. Dave thought this manoeuvre was hilarious and whooped loudly but, in the back, Poppy was thrown across the floor and would have collided with the rear doors had the chain not held her in place. As Dave steadied the van, she noticed that even her unknown companion had slipped across the floor to a new position slightly further away from her. Nonetheless, she remained alert and listened to the now-familiar rumbling noises beneath the floor.

The van was moving fast, and, every so often, the whole structure banged and bounced over uneven surfaces on the road. Although Poppy felt groggy and very fearful, she was not about to give in to tyranny. No one was going to dominate her. The small dog needed to concentrate if she was to find a solution to her present predicament. As she became more aware of her physical situation, her thoughts returned to the dull ache in her leg where Dave had, quite viciously, jabbed something sharp into her flesh. In addition, the harness to which the chain was attached had chafed her skin and was causing a lot of pain.

Poppy was utterly drained, both mentally and physically, which made it extremely difficult for her to remain alert and examine her situation. She keenly felt the frustration and anguish of events that seemed to be spiralling out of her control. After much contemplation, she stretched out on the floor and succumbed to her exhaustion, no longer able to worry about her potential nemesis, sprawled out only feet from where she lay.

Meanwhile, the van with all its occupants continued on its way.

Approximately two hours later, Poppy woke from a deep sleep, still disorientated and with no ability to think clearly. This was extremely unusual because Lhasa's have earned a reputation as alert and competent watchdogs. Although consumed by anxiety, Poppy tried hard to keep her wits about her, particularly when the mysterious creature moved again and Poppy heard the metallic sound of a chain scraping on the floor. Until that moment, it had not occurred to her that this creature might also be shackled. This simple fact made her feel more secure. After all, not even the fiercest animal can bite through a strong chain.

Suddenly, and without warning, the van pulled up sharply. Poppy had been about to doze off again but was now vigilant and ready for anything. Seconds later, the doors opened, and Bernie, torch in hand, clambered into the space. Coughing and wheezing, he aimed the beam directly into her eyes. Although temporarily blinded, Poppy attempted to escape, but the short chain held firm, and the human merely laughed derisively. Poppy looked up at him with disgust. He was definitely not to be trusted. Outside the van, Dave called in to him.

"What's happening, Bernie?"

"The big one's still out cold, Dave. I definitely gave it too much."

"Grey's not going to be happy, mate. Let's stick to the plan and get back late, cos I wouldn't want to be in your shoes if he finds out what you did."

Dave remained outside watching his friend tend to the unconscious animal on the floor. Poppy didn't really understand their conversation but had a feeling that they were not talking about her. Just then, Dave jumped up into the van and looked around. After restoring the overturned bowl to its former position, he filled it to the brim using the water bottle in his hand. Spurred on by a reckless impulse, Poppy lunged forward and tried to bite Bernie but was halted by the chain. Dave raised his hand to strike the little dog, but Poppy pulled away just as Bernie grabbed Dave's arm.

"No, Dave! We're in enough trouble as it is. Leave it."

Dave apologised but with contempt. "Just trying to protect you, mate."

It seemed clear to Poppy that the men were extremely anxious about the condition of the unconscious animal as they knelt on the floor, talking to each other in hushed tones. Cowering in the darkness, Poppy became increasingly disturbed by the sound of this animal, gasping for air and apparently fighting for its life, and she tried to get a better view. Unfortunately, the humans were directly in her line of sight, which made it extremely difficult to see very much at all. Suddenly, however, the smaller man moved slightly to his left, which enabled Poppy to see a bloodied cloth wound tightly around his right hand. Eventually, the two men clambered down from the back of the van and slammed the doors. A few seconds later, the vehicle resumed its noisy, erratic progress.

Poppy was now desperately thirsty and decided to take a drink, even though it ran counter to her better judgement. She was normally suspicious of everything but just couldn't help herself. She looked across and listened carefully. Something was terribly wrong because her fellow captive had been asleep for hours now, and this concerned and unsettled her. This was a very large animal, and Poppy could not understand how these two humans had managed to capture it so easily. Just then, her thoughts focused on the ugly little man and the red patches staining the material wrapped around his fingers. Perhaps it had been a more difficult undertaking after all. Then she had another thought — any enemy of these humans had to be her friend.

Chapter Four

The Compound

It was just before half-past nine in the evening when Dave Dixon arrived at his destination and manoeuvred the van through an open security gate. A weather-beaten board attached to the main entrance identified the place as 'Grey's Dog Rescue Centre'. While Bernie closed the gate, Dave drove carefully down the gravelled drive and parked the vehicle in one of the four spaces directly in front of a rather grand but neglected country house. The former manor and its substantial grounds were completely enclosed by a wire fence at least eight feet high.

A second gate lay open, providing access to the garden area comprising approximately two acres of land within which there was a large wooden barn flanked by two smaller sheds set about twelve feet apart. The former garden had once boasted a well-kept lawn complete with trees and flower beds, although that had been many seasons ago. All that remained of its glory days were one or two small patches of grass and two concrete gargoyles attached to what was left of a low brick wall.

Dave had just clambered out of the van when a silver-haired gentleman approached him. This was Charles Grey, one of the individuals responsible for this criminal enterprise. He was in his early sixties, tall, thin and elegantly dressed. He possessed an aura of authority, and his smart appearance and quietly spoken manner concealed a stone-hearted and ruthless nature.

He had purchased the house some two years ago as its isolated position and extensive grounds had suited his illicit purpose. Charles was cold and unemotional and thought of profit rather than the welfare of the unfortunate animals held captive in this unhappy place.

Both Dave and Bernie had a healthy respect for their employer and usually did as they were told, fully aware of his violent reputation. It seemed the sensible thing to do. In his youth, Charles, who had grown up in London's East End, had spent time in one of Her Majesty's Detention Centres for various violent offences. He had since managed to remain at liberty by employing others to do his dirty work — for a price. Aided by his wife Joan, he managed the business, which involved the theft and subsequent sale of dogs, usually to selected clients looking for a particular breed. To Charles, this was low-level criminal activity offering very little chance of apprehension. Even if the police tried to charge him with anything, he knew that one of his minions would step up and take the blame. The man was also aware that fewer than five percent of such cases resulted in a conviction. Considering the money he was making, he calculated that it was a risk worth taking.

Grey was the first to speak, but the tone of his voice lacked warmth.

"How'd it go, Dave?"

"We got both of them, Mr Grey," the younger man replied, surprised that his boss was still about. "It all went pretty well overall." Dave's voice caught briefly. "They're, er, a bit groggy at the moment, but it won't take long to settle them in. Do you want to know when they're ready?"

Grey studied Dave carefully for a few seconds and nodded. "You're late back. Any problems?"

Dave, suddenly aware that he was being closely scrutinised, tried to sound as confident as possible. "There's nothing you need to worry about, boss."

Grey continued to stare intently at him, then appeared to accept his summary of the day's events without further question. He turned and ambled nonchalantly back to the house. Dave looked over at his mate and gave him the thumbs up. Bernie looked extremely uneasy but managed an anxious smile before returning to his duties.

Once Charles was back in the house, the two men set about getting the new arrivals into the nearest shed so that they could more easily assess their condition.

Both men fervently hoped that the ailing dog would come round quickly once settled into a more comfortable environment. Bernie first detached Poppy's lead from the clip in the floor and then encouraged her to jump out of the van. It was much cooler now, and the small dog shivered a little as she adjusted to the night air. She tried to study her surroundings but couldn't see much in the darkness apart from a huge metal gate and a very high fence.

Bernie opened the door to the shed, switched on a light and then pulled the reluctant Lhasa inside. Looking around, Poppy noticed two makeshift beds, which consisted of wooden boards, each covered by a thin layer of straw. Once the little dog was in place, Bernie secured her to a metal clip attached to a wooden rail. Dave then carefully placed two large bowls on the floor, one containing water and the other some sort of food. Poppy needed both, although, after a quick taste, she found the water to be lukewarm and the food stale. Only a matter of days ago, she would not have touched any of it, but things were different now. To preserve her strength and to remain alert to any chance of escape, she had no choice but to take advantage of whatever rations these criminal humans provided.

A few moments later, a struggling Dave carried the second dog into the shed and placed him on the other bed before securing his chain to the nearby rail. After Dave had departed and closed the door, Poppy took the time to study her new surroundings while the rather dim light, swinging gently just above her head, remained on. Although there no longer appeared to be an immediate threat to her safety, she still needed to know with whom she was sharing this cramped space. She strained against her chain with as much force as she could muster, and this seemed to loosen the rusty clip attached to her collar. On subsequent attempts to break free, Poppy forced herself forward and then, with the chain under pressure, twisted and turned her body this way and that until the clip gave way and split into two separate pieces. The small dog was free but, worried that she might have been heard, hurriedly settled back on her bed.

Seated on the straw, Poppy pricked up her ears and listened intently, but nothing stirred, and she sensed no danger. This boosted her confidence, and so she edged slowly and cautiously toward the unconscious animal. A sudden noise from outside the building startled Poppy, and she froze, one paw lifted and with her ears on full alert. After a few seconds, the silence returned, and she continued her tentative approach. As her travelling companion slowly came into focus, it became clear that this animal was just another dog, although one of enormous size. His breathing was laboured, and the dog groaned occasionally, even though still fast asleep. Poppy began to relax and thought herself foolish to have feared this creature so much. Back home, she was friendly with a Great Dane, and this dog looked very much the same although much more powerful.

Poppy spoke to her companion gently, but the dog didn't stir and remained in what appeared to be an unusually deep sleep. If it were possible to escape from these men, she felt sure that a dog like this would be an invaluable partner. Ever watchful, she lay down beside what she hoped would be a new friend and ally, although she remained mindful of the need to keep her wits about her. With this in mind, she returned to her own bed and sprawled out on the straw. It was a very quiet night. As she lay there and focused her thoughts on the day's life-changing events, she heard what sounded like dogs pacing around the yard just outside the shed door. She sensed that there were two of them, apparently free to wander around at will. She wondered who they were and what they were actually doing. A black depression settled over Poppy as she contemplated everything that had led, inexorably, to her incarceration in this awful place. Snatched away from her home by violent humans, she had been callously thrown into their van without a thought for her health or well-being. As a result, she had received injuries, not only when her head had slammed into the solid metal floor of the vehicle but also from the sharp instrument that had been savagely thrust into her hind leg.

Shortly before midnight, Poppy woke to the sound of footsteps crunching across the gravel. The door opened, and Charles and Joan slipped silently into the shed, having just been made aware of the Great Dane's condition. It seemed that, after further questioning from Grey, Dave had broken his silence and told his employer everything, thus ensuring that he would not be implicated should the dog not survive. On this occasion, Bernie would have to accept responsibility for his own actions. Poppy sensed an atmosphere as the elderly couple crouched over the unconscious animal and talked quietly to each other, clearly concerned.

"Phone the girl tonight, Joan. Maybe she can help. I know it's late but get her in early tomorrow." Charles looked worried.

"Alright, Charlie, I will, but do me a favour. Sort Bernie out." Joan appeared to be furious. "This animal is valuable, and that moron could've killed it. His negligence might still cost us. Get Frank to teach him a lesson he won't forget!"

Charles was reluctant to involve Frank Wilson, one of his old mates from the East End, because the dog appeared to be recovering, so no real harm had been done. Yes, Bernie had let him down, no doubt about that, but he was loyal, and Charles trusted him. The problem was that Joan despised Bernie and had been looking for a reason to sack him for some time now.

"Okay, love. I'll talk to Frank but let this be the end of it. There's to be no more talk of getting rid. Right?"

Charles looked directly at his wife and, satisfied that she would leave the matter to him, left the shed. Joan was an equal partner in the business but far more cunning than her husband, making her the driving force behind their success. She had a cruel side to her nature and disliked dogs of any size or breed. In fact, this woman disliked any animal unfortunate enough to cross her path. To her, these terrified dogs were just a commodity to be sold on to others for the maximum profit. In common with her husband, she too had been brought up amongst criminals and, whilst fully aware that their business was illegal, couldn't have cared less.

Whilst preoccupied with the Great Dane, Joan was not aware that Poppy was awake. When she turned her head, Poppy just pretended to be asleep, something she was rather good at. After taking a last look at the unconscious animal, now breathing normally, Joan walked quietly over to Poppy. Still feigning sleep, the small dog remained motionless while this heartless old woman stared at her. Naturally, the little Lhasa kept the loose end of the lead hidden beneath her body and, after only a few minutes, Joan walked out of the shed, leaving the little dog alone again.

Since being confined in this place, Poppy had been unable to allow herself the rest her exhausted mind and body craved. What sleep she had managed to snatch had been fitful and of no real benefit, leaving her feeling tired and irritable. It was different now. She took one last look at the slumbering giant, then laid her head gently onto the straw and closed her eyes. The darkness simply overwhelmed her, and she drifted into a deep, undisturbed sleep.

Hours passed in peaceful dreams of friendly faces calling her home. Much later, the sound of voices interrupted Poppy's slumber, and she looked around, surprised to find herself completely alone. She surmised that the bad humans must have come in during the early hours and taken her friend away. The sun was shining through the half-open door, allowing her to see the interior of the shed quite clearly. No doubt, those holding her captive had assumed she was properly secured by her chain and had left the door ajar when they removed her fellow prisoner. Poppy thought briefly about escape but was smart enough to know that it was probably inadvisable for now. Moreover, this course of action would mean leaving her huge companion behind, and she couldn't do that. Thrown together by circumstances beyond their control, they might need each other if they were to attempt to get away.

Poppy recognised the need to develop an escape plan although, after further consideration, realised that she needed far more information about what lay beyond the shed. She concluded that all thoughts of escape must be shelved for the time being and that her strategy should include scouting out the ground beyond her place of confinement. After that, it would be sensible to communicate with any other animals that might be confined with her in an effort to gather as much intelligence as possible. A quick examination of her own surroundings and her acute sense of smell detected the scent of dogs long gone from this place. There were chains affixed to a rail that ran around the perimeter of the shed, which had almost certainly been used to constrain them.

It disturbed Poppy to think that she was not the only dog to have been torn away from a loving home by these despicable men. Continuing her inspection, Poppy approached the half-open door and poked her head through the narrow gap to get a better look. The first thing to catch her eye was her new friend, limping slowly around the compound, accompanied by the ugly little man responsible for her own kidnap. Poppy was so relieved to see the Great Dane on his feet that she almost yelped with joy, but common sense prevailed. It was clear to her that this powerful dog, slowly recuperating from the treatment meted out by the seemingly heartless Bernie, still needed help and support. Nevertheless, standing defiantly on the concrete, this dog looked magnificent and even bigger than Poppy had supposed while both had been chained in the van.

The second thing Poppy saw was a cat, but it was in no sense an ordinary cat. This particular animal was staring right back at her. Of course, a cat with a bit of an attitude staring at a dog is not unusual in itself, but there was something else about this dark brown feline that Poppy couldn't quite comprehend. Try as she might, she couldn't shake the feeling that it was trying to engage with her in some way. Without thinking, Poppy had accidentally stepped out into the open. The sound of Bernie's raised voice startled both animals, who turned their heads in his direction just in time to see him strike the helpless Great Dane on the side of the head. This may have been retribution for what the powerful beast had done to Bernie the previous day, but, nonetheless, it angered the cat, whose tail was now flicking from side to side in quiet fury.

Poppy felt compelled to act and stepped out into the yard ready and willing to aid her stricken companion, but, to Poppy's astonishment, the mysterious feline stood up, glared at her fiercely and then shook her head. Shocked and confused, she jumped back inside the shed.

After composing herself, Poppy ventured cautiously back into the yard, but the cat was no longer in sight.

Chapter Five

A Friend on the Inside

Jean Sparrow, the young lady employed by the Greys as a kennel worker, normally started her shift around seven in the morning although, very late the previous night, she had received a telephone call from Joan Grey requesting a much earlier start. Jean, who had been in bed at the time, was none too happy about this sudden change of routine but, unfortunately, she couldn't object because out of hours working formed part of her job description and she dared not refuse. Indeed, the Greys weren't the sort of people to accept anything less than total compliance. Jean normally walked to work, a journey of about a mile if she took the shortcut across the meadow. It was a lovely walk when the weather was fine and made her feel so much better about her life which had dramatically changed for the worse over the last few months. During periods when it was cold and wet or when she was needed urgently, she would drive in. Today was one of those times.

According to Mrs Grey, one of two new arrivals was very poorly and struggling to breathe, symptoms that would normally have involved the services of a veterinary surgeon. However, Jean had been working at the rescue centre for at least two months and had never seen a vet even though there had been one or two quite serious issues during that time. Experience told her that the treatment for this dog would be left to her. Although she was not fully qualified, having spent only two years in veterinary college, she had gained a good deal of nursing knowledge in that time.

Jean had been forced to quit college abruptly without completing the course because her grandmother had developed a serious illness and needed to be looked after at home. Without hesitation, the young woman had agreed to move in with her gran and provide the required care for as long as it was necessary, thus putting her career on hold for the foreseeable future. The job at the rescue centre was not ideal, but she had to support herself during this difficult period. Jean had reservations about the Greys but could not overlook the advantages of a local job with working hours that suited her current needs. Moreover, she loved working with animals, particularly dogs.

Once she arrived at the yard, she took over from Bernie and walked with the Great Dane for a further two circuits of the compound to assess his condition. From the information displayed on the metal disc attached to his collar, she learned that the dog's name was Brutus, although the owner's address and phone number had been deliberately removed. This was a classic sign of an abandoned or stolen dog, as Jean knew only too well. Apparently, Brutus had woken up in the early hours of the morning in a distressed state, having been unconscious for hours. One of Grey's lackeys, a cruel and callous individual by the name of Bernie French, had managed to get the dog on its feet and out of the shed, but it was still very groggy and only just able to walk. As she was examining the dog, Charles Grey came out of the house and stood beside her.

"What's the problem, Jeannie?" Her employer enquired.

Jean felt a little flustered and very nervous under Grey's intense gaze. "This dog seems to have been heavily sedated, Mr Grey. He's confused and unsteady on his feet. I might be wrong, but it looks like an overdose to me."

Jean was aware of the anxiety in her voice and struggled to keep her emotions under control. She knew that this place wasn't quite what it seemed but felt it wise to keep her own counsel and, more importantly, she needed this job. In spite of her reservations, Jean was aware that the Greys had connections with a lot of people, including pet shop owners and a number of private individuals, willing to provide a safe home for a rescued dog. The problem for Jean was that, judging from her limited experience, she could not detect any real signs of abandonment or inhumane treatment at all. Victims of abuse, neglect and abandonment usually display all sorts of problems, both mental and physical. These dogs were in exceptionally good condition and appeared to have no behavioural issues. For example, barring his current drowsiness, the Great Dane had been groomed recently, possibly within the last few weeks. Jean could not make any sense of it.

The young woman's concentration was suddenly broken by a sound just outside the shed, and she looked in that direction. Surprisingly, standing only a few feet away, unsecured and staring straight at her, was a young Lhasa apso.

"Is that the other new arrival, Mr Grey?" Jean enquired politely.

Charles was uncharacteristically friendly in his response. "Yes, Jeannie. Came in yesterday with the Great Dane. Bernie was supposed to secure it in the shed last night but clearly messed up yet again. You take care of the animals. I'll deal with Bernie."

Jean didn't like Bernie much, but then she didn't like Charles Grey either, so she just did as she was told and attended to her young charges. Whatever was going on in this dreadful place, she would always look out for the dogs.

Meanwhile, deep in thought, Poppy realised that she had inadvertently slipped through the door into the yard, making herself visible to everyone else. She looked around nervously, instantly aware that a much younger lady, one she hadn't seen before, was staring at her. Poppy had been caught out and had no idea what to do. The young woman looked very surprised to see her.

"Good girl," she said. "Stay there, and I'll bring you something nice."

Jean walked over to where Poppy was standing and gently stroked her fur. Poppy was surprised and really pleased because it was the first act of kindness she had experienced since being thrown into that filthy van. The young woman reached into her pocket for something, and Poppy jumped back instinctively although, when Jean opened her hand, she revealed only a savoury treat. The little dog really wanted it but didn't respond immediately because she simply didn't know who to trust anymore. After all that had happened, Poppy remained suspicious of this new human. Jean studied the metal disc, still attached to Poppy's harness.

"I'm very pleased to meet you, Poppy. My name is Jean." She smiled and looked deep into Poppy's eyes. "Don't look so surprised. You're still wearing your name tag. It's alright. If you don't want the treat now, you can have it later. Nobody will harm you, I promise. I'm your friend and will take very good care of you. You're quite safe with me."

The young lady's easy-going manner, open face and soothing voice helped the small dog to relax and control her fear. Over Jean's shoulder, she recognised the tall human from the day before. His manner seemed cold and unpleasant, although Poppy appeared to be the only one to sense it. While the young woman was talking, he smiled at her kindly, even though his eyes did not reflect any warmth. Poppy judged his amiable demeanour to be entirely false.

"Jean, take the Lhasa apso back to the shed and make sure she can't get free this time. Put her with the others tomorrow."

"Yes, Mr Grey," Jean replied curtly. "What about the other one? He needs to be properly checked out."

"Alright, Jean. You win." Charles lied to her face. "I'll give the vet a call. Mind you, the dog's looking a whole lot better now, thanks to your efforts. Just put him in the shed with the Lhasa. You can keep an eye on him there." Jean suspected that Charles was just fobbing her off, but what could she do? She watched as he strolled back to the house and shuddered with revulsion. Jean was rapidly becoming convinced that, far from being rescued, the dogs in her care were more likely to have been stolen. She turned her attention back to Brutus, struggling to stay on his feet, and questioned how this animal had come to be in this awful physical state in the first place. There was a tear in her eye as she cuddled Poppy, who returned her affection by licking the young

47

woman's hand. Jean was unable to rid herself of the belief that this beautiful little dog might have been ill-treated by these people. Sadly, she doubted that the Greys would interest themselves in any dog's future happiness or welfare. She led Poppy back into the shed and carefully attached another chain to her harness. She then gently patted Poppy's head and put the treat down for her to have at another time.

A few moments later, Jean helped the unsteady Great Dane into the shed and secured him in place right next to Poppy. She also adjusted both chains to allow the two animals to move about with less restraint. This kindness enabled both dogs to stretch their legs and drink from the bowl of water in the middle of the floor.

As Jean quietly left the shed, she looked back and smiled: "Bye, Poppy. Bye, Brutus. I'll bring you some food shortly and make sure you're both okay."

After the unhappy pair were left alone, Brutus stood up gingerly and, taking advantage of the greater freedom of movement made possible by Jean, tottered over towards Poppy, where he introduced himself. He truly was a giant but still looked very shaky. When they were both settled, he began to tell his story.

"I've been very foolish, Poppy," Brutus whispered. He seemed to be very upset. "I lived on a farm and had the run of the place. On the day I was taken, I saw two humans standing by an old van in the bottom field. I thought that they were up to no good, so I trotted over to investigate. As I approached, one of the men held out his hand as if he was my friend, so I relaxed. Unwisely, I didn't think I was in any danger and let my guard down, which allowed him to attach a chain to my collar. There was this beautiful smell in the air coming from the van, and, foolishly, I let the human lead me inside. Then, before I could react, the brute jumped out and slammed the doors shut. Immediately after that, the van started moving. I was trapped, and that made me very angry. You were there too, Poppy, but you were asleep on the floor, completely oblivious to what was happening. My only thought was to escape, and I tried to fight my way out. Unfortunately, even though I gave the doors a good hammering, I was forced to admit defeat and accepted that I needed to play a waiting game. I kicked the bowls over and sat at the back, waiting for them to come for me — it didn't take long! The van stopped, and one of those barbarians opened the doors. As the first one climbed in, I attacked him and knocked him out of the van. Unfortunately, while I was dealing with one human, the other stabbed something into my leg. It really hurt, and I bit his hand as hard as I could. There was a lot of blood. After that, I don't remember anything until I woke up in this shed."

"They did something to you, Brutus," Poppy said. "Whatever it was must have knocked you out because you took ages to wake up again, and the humans

49

became extremely concerned. Now, I don't know who these people are or what they want with us, but I do know that we have to get away from here."

Just then, the shed door opened, and Jean walked back in with two bowls of food. Brutus and Poppy were still wary even though the meal looked delicious. Jean sat down between them with one hand on Poppy and the other on Brutus.

"What's the matter with the pair of you?" She seemed quite upset that they wouldn't eat the food. "What's happened to you that you just won't eat? Look at me now." With that, Jean took a small morsel of food from each bowl and put them both in her mouth. "Oh! Lovely," she said." Now it's your turn."

Poppy observed Jean's face and sensed love and kindness. Usually, a Lhasa apso wouldn't easily trust a stranger, but she was ravenous and gave in fairly quickly. Brutus, on the other hand, held out for a while longer, at least until hunger overcame his fear. Then he looked at Jean and ate the food. Jean was not like the others; Poppy was sure of that. Maybe this human wasn't aware of the cruelty inflicted on them by Bernie and his friends, but they both felt at ease in her company and agreed to trust her in future.

In the afternoon, Bernie entered the shed, closely followed by Dave, who released both dogs. On this occasion, Bernie, well aware that Brutus was regaining his strength, stood well back and let Dave take the Great Dane's leash. Dave laughed and called the older man a coward as he led Brutus outside. The huge dog growled at both his captors but behaved himself on this occasion. Bernie grasped Poppy's lead and followed his friend outside, where Charles Grey greeted them as they emerged from the shed.

"Glad to see you awake, Brutus. You had us worried for a while."

As the old man was speaking, he noticed that Bernie was shuffling his feet and staring down at the ground. Grey was incensed that this idiot had messed up twice, first by overdoing the sedative injected into the Great Dane and then by failing to properly secure the Lhasa. Although he had some reservations, Grey felt that, taking all things into consideration, Bernie needed a few helpful and memorable reminders regarding his work practices.

He was quiet for a moment, but then, turning his thoughts back to Brutus and Poppy, he continued his welcome speech. "Today, I'm going to let you both into your new home and introduce you to some friends."

This was all lies, of course, and though Poppy had no idea what Grey had just said, she wasn't fooled by his unusually pleasant manner. At the time, the only question in her mind was how all these humans came to know her name.

Chapter Six

An Extraordinary Cat

The atmosphere inside the shed that afternoon had been oppressive, and Poppy and Brutus were both relieved to be outside in the cooler air. In the centre of the compound, there were two huge bowls containing food and water surrounded by a small number of unfamiliar dogs who appeared to be friendly and approachable. Dave was clearly worried about permitting Brutus to mix with these animals, but he had been given his instructions and was not about to cause problems. As he unclipped the Great Dane's lead, leaving Brutus completely free, Dave worried that an aggressive dog like this could easily unsettle the others and create mayhem in the process.

The Great Dane was three years old and very opinionated and intolerant, as well as holding fixed and closed-minded views on all manner of subjects. He was a very powerful animal with a muscular physique matched by an enormous ego. Predominantly light brown in colour, Brutus' ears and muzzle were black, and he sported a large white patch on his chest. Loyal and kind but extremely bad-tempered at times, he was accustomed to getting his own way. This attitude often made him appear spoiled and entitled. Reckless by nature, Brutus would never walk away from a fight and would stand up to any opponent without fear. In Poppy's opinion, he would make a truly loyal friend but would never be a deep thinker or a schemer.

The young Lhasa apso glanced to her left and watched as the huge dog, relishing his freedom, strode arrogantly into the compound area. Simultaneously, Bernie unclipped Poppy's lead and allowed her the luxury of exploring her surroundings and making herself known to the other captive canines. In this endeavour, it was vital not to alert the bellicose-looking sentries standing just inside the gate. As the two friends moved forward, both guard dogs stared at Brutus, almost daring him to start trouble. Their overall demeanour worried Poppy more than a little, and wisely, she stopped and turned away. Unfortunately, it had the opposite effect on Brutus, who suddenly halted, pawed the ground, and stared straight back at them defiantly.

Any other opponents would have backed off faced with such a threat, but as Brutus approached them, the two guard dogs gave him a menacing look and strode forward to confront him. Any altercation at this early stage worried Poppy greatly because she needed to keep a low profile while she prepared her escape plan. Any challenge to the hierarchy could prove to be an absolute disaster and might scupper any attempt to break out of their prison. Unhappily, Poppy had not had the opportunity to discuss anything with Brutus and was unable to influence this event. The headstrong Great Dane was in his element and revelled in the prospect of a fight. His two adversaries could not match him in size, but both looked tough enough to deal with a potential troublemaker. Poppy understood very well that they should not be underestimated. There was a very brief conversation between the three animals before Brutus returned to Poppy's side.

"I've seen mutts like this before, Poppy. They're Doberman pinschers, tough dogs, but friendly enough when you get to know them. The trouble is that this pair are different — nasty specimens, expressly trained to be ruthless. You must be very careful when they're around."

"Your words of caution seem very sensible, Brutus," Poppy replied sincerely, "but I'm not the one they're worried about. You are. They see you as a problem for the simple reason that you aren't afraid of them. Please be smart and steer clear of these Dobermans if you can because, if you do not, it will ruin everything. Anyway, what did they say to you?"

"Apart from what I've already told you, not very much," Brutus replied casually. "Just that they are fighting dogs, and there are two of them. They're tasked with making us subservient — fat chance! And, of course, ensuring there aren't any escapes. They're brothers, by the way."

After taking refreshment, Poppy strolled around the compound, talking to some of the other inmates and asking for their stories. It didn't take long to establish that all those currently held in this place had been snatched from their owners within the last few weeks. Some had already been removed from the compound in the same van that Poppy had arrived in. Only eight remained, including Brutus and Poppy. Just then, Lester, one of the Doberman brothers, trotted over and tried to break up the conversation. Brutus stood firm, and the guard dog backed down.

Poppy supposed that this conversation wasn't worth fighting over, but the Doberman sidled over to his brother, and they both glared at Brutus, who just stared straight back. It was clear to Poppy that Brutus had to curb his natural aggression, however difficult that might be. Moreover, she felt it was imperative that she keep an eye on him.

That evening, before being returned to the shed, Poppy was sitting alone by the wire fence gazing longingly out to the fields beyond. To her left, the landscape consisted of open fields and meadowland stretching as far as the eye could see. It was a truly beautiful sight. Looking to her right, across the narrow lane and towards a large area of scrubland, she could clearly make out the boundaries of what appeared to be a huge forest, dark and foreboding. It made the little dog tremble just thinking about what perils lay within the trees.

This was an evil and desolate place, and Poppy didn't want to be here any longer than necessary. It was imperative, therefore, that any escape had to be organised very quickly. She just didn't yet know how this might be achieved. Again, her thoughts turned to the warmth and kindness of her parents and her beautiful home. It saddened Poppy immensely that she might never see her family again. Her feelings of pain and sorrow, however, acted as motivation to invest all her energy and ability in an attempt to break out of this place and take all the other dogs with her.

"Poppy."

She heard her name called and turned towards the sound. She spotted Jean, who was clutching a lead in one hand and beckoning her forward with the other.

Poppy despised these people because they had stolen her wonderful life without heed for her feelings. She still didn't know if Jean was one of the bad humans or not, but this lady treated all the captives with kindness and respect and, for that, deserved the benefit of the doubt. Just before Poppy trotted over to greet her, she took one last look at the fields beyond the prison. There was a movement in the long grass about two feet inside the wire fence. When she focused on the spot, she could hardly believe her eyes because there it was again, the mysterious cat sitting as bold as brass inside the compound. Poppy had no idea what was going on. Was it possible that this feline belonged to the criminals responsible for their plight? If so, any attempt to escape might be more likely to fail. Instead of an ally, this cat may be a spy. Poppy jumped as Jean suddenly appeared next to her and clipped on her lead. She had no choice but to go into the shed with her but, just before they got to the door, she looked back. The cat was no longer visible.

That night, Poppy felt deflated because this intriguing feline had given her cause to hope. If this animal was somehow connected to her enemies, it would be devastating to the young dog and add to the many difficulties she would face when attempting to secure her freedom plus that of all her fellow captives. Poppy decided to confide in Brutus and ask for his opinion. After all, she was not compelled to take his advice, whatever that might be. Unfortunately, Brutus was predictably dismissive. In his opinion, dogs should never trust cats and must exercise the greatest care when dealing with such creatures. According to him, this feline probably lived in the house with the humans and would end up betraying her and any other dog foolish enough to become a part of her escape plan. Poppy liked

Brutus because he had a generous heart and would almost certainly look after her in the future, but she also felt strongly that he was wrong. Brutus was tough enough, all right, but he was not smart.

After hearing what the Great Dane had to say, Poppy looked the bigger dog straight in the eye and asked him why he was so against the idea of escape.

"Brutus, we have no way of knowing how awful our future will be if we stay here trapped in this nightmare. I don't have a clue how to get away from this place, with or without the help of a cat, but I believe I have to try."

"What are you thinking, Poppy?" Brutus replied in an exasperated manner. "How can a solitary cat get you out of here, never mind about the rest of us? It also makes me suspicious of this animal anyway. Why would a cat be bothered about the fate of a handful of dogs? That makes no sense."

Poppy nodded. "You may be right, Brutus, but if you are, it means I have to give up my dream of returning home to my family, and I just can't do that. This cat wants to speak to me, I'm sure, so if you don't mind, I'll carry on scheming."

"Well, Poppy, you know what I think, and as far as I am concerned, that's that."

Brutus looked down on Poppy for a few long seconds, then wheeled around and walked over to his bed, where he made himself comfortable. He was not a happy dog. Poppy suddenly became aware of loud snoring and realised that her companion had fallen into a deep sleep. She lay there in the fading light as a sense of desolation threatened to overwhelm her. Brutus saw her only as a small and insignificant dog that needed constant care and attention.

Nevertheless, Poppy knew that she must stand firm and not let anything interfere with her resolve to engineer an escape. If she wanted to get back to her home and parents again, she had to remain alert to every single opportunity and be ready to do whatever was necessary to get away from this hideous place. For that, a clear mind would be needed — and plenty of good luck.

Chapter Seven

Where There Is a Will

All dogs need a lot of rest, and Poppy and Brutus were no exceptions. Without sufficient sleep, animals become more aggressive, anxious and stressed. Since her kidnap, only two days previously, Poppy had found it extremely difficult to relax and would doze intermittently throughout the night.

On this particular morning, however, something had disturbed her fitful slumber. She silently rose to her feet, growled softly and pricked up her ears in an attempt to divine the source of her strong feelings of anxiety. The peaceful atmosphere inside the small shed contrasted with two strident female voices coming from the compound gate close to the house. She glanced across at Brutus and noticed that he was still sound asleep and snoring quietly. Little appeared to disturb the Great Dane. Without giving her companion a second thought, she decided to investigate the matter on her own and positioned herself close to a small aperture in the shed door. Although her view was limited, she could just make out the old lady from the big house wagging her finger at somebody she could not see. She turned back to the sleeping Brutus but chose not to wake him at that time because he had developed a very bad habit of interfering in her affairs and then lecturing her on the rights and wrongs of any subject, including those he knew nothing about. Although he was physically intimidating and very strong, he had little experience of life in the wild.

As far as Brutus was concerned, the captive dogs had little or no chance of ever returning to their previous lives and should, therefore, accept the inevitable. He had a naive view of life and honestly believed that everything would turn out right in the end. Poppy refused to countenance this defeatist view and would never yield to the tyranny imposed on the dogs by these callous humans. Ultimately, if she followed her friend's advice, it would mean giving up on any chance of returning to her family and friends and accepting that she would never see her home again. This would effectively condemn her to a life of heartache and loss.

Poppy's attention returned to the voices in the yard outside, which now sounded less acrimonious and not quite so loud. This reassured the little dog, but she still wondered who might walk through the door and for what purpose. Although fearful and uncertain, she managed to overcome all her negative impulses and seize the initiative by utilising her inner strength. Every time she experienced these episodes of weakness and doubt, Poppy always felt ashamed of herself. She firmly believed that, whatever was to happen in the future, she must always fight this injustice. Her thoughts centred on the mysterious feline that had been skulking inside the wire fence and could have been trying to make contact with her. That was extraordinary in itself. The Lhasa apso was no lover of cats, although she couldn't quite pinpoint the reason for this attitude. Brutus had told her that a cat needs watching all the time, but she had an instinct about this one and was certain that it didn't belong to the criminal humans. If a cat really was trying to help her, she had to be ready the next time it turned up.

Returning to the disturbance in the yard, Poppy could still hear human voices outside the shed door, although she had no conception of what was being said. One of the voices was Jean's, and the other definitely belonged to the grey-haired lady from the day before. The door was still closed, making it impossible to see anyone in the yard, but Poppy sensed that the older lady had been very angry with Jean. For the time being, however, things seemed to have calmed down.

There was a brief period of silence before the door opened, and Jean walked in with breakfast.

"Good morning, Poppy. Good morning, Brutus. Come and get your breakfast because it's going to be a very busy day. Some of the dogs are being taken to their new homes this morning."

On hearing Jean's voice, Brutus stirred and looked round, genuinely pleased to see her. After putting down the food, the young woman sat down between the two friends with one arm around Poppy and the other around the Great Dane.

"I'm sorry, Poppy, but you and Brutus are going to be separated today."

Jean looked upset as she continued. "It's not my idea, but I'm afraid that Brutus is staying here, and you are moving into the barn with the other dogs. I disagreed with the decision to split you up, but Mrs Grey was adamant. I don't like it any more than you do, but I have to do as I'm told." Then she whispered in Poppy's ear. "This place isn't right, Poppy, but I'll try to look after you. Trust me when I tell you that nothing is what it seems. I've had no difficulty reaching that conclusion."

Poppy stared back at Jean, not comprehending what had just been said. In common with other dogs, she was able to read human facial expressions and understand many of their words. Poppy could even distinguish between the different tones in which such words were delivered but, sadly, couldn't fully grasp the meaning behind them. Nonetheless, it was evident to Poppy that the news was not good.

After the two dogs had eaten, Jean clipped on their leads and took them outside. Poppy expected a quick walk around the yard but was taken through the second gate into the rectangular area where she had met the other dogs the day before. She looked around and caught sight of her two human enemies once again.

Dave and Bernie were attempting to pacify three young golden retrievers and get them into the back of their van. Inevitably, because the dogs were anxious and very frightened, the men were struggling. Jean was quick to assess the problem and ran over to help. She cuddled all of the dogs in turn and then encouraged each one into the van. Dave really liked Jean and, in her presence, tried hard to conceal his true nature.

While he observed Jean, Poppy kept a suspicious eye on him. Surely, it must have been obvious to anyone who had witnessed this scene that these dogs were terrified. Poppy had not yet had an opportunity to speak to any one of them but firmly believed they had suffered kidnap and imprisonment in exactly the same way that she had.

Once the retrievers had been secured, the doors of the van were closed, and it moved slowly away. So intently had Poppy been watching this scene that she hadn't noticed another dog sidle up to her. The new arrival was Nina, a Siberian husky who looked pretty tough. After introducing herself, Poppy asked Nina to tell her more about the compound and how long the dogs had been imprisoned in this place. The husky appeared to be in a bad mood and answered her in a very aggressive way.

"Listen. I don't know you, and I don't see the point in talking to you. I've been in this rathole for two weeks now, and most of the dogs who were here when I arrived have gone. The three you just watched being taken away had been here for about three weeks which seems to be the maximum stay for any of us."

"Do you know anything about a cat, Nina?" Poppy asked politely.

"Absolutely nothing. Poppy, did you say? You might like to talk to Flora and Millie over there because they saw an unusual cat only the other day. Mind you, this is a very unusual place."

Poppy glanced at the two dogs mentioned and made a mental note to talk to both of them as soon as possible.

"All I can tell you, Poppy," Nina added coldly, "is that two dogs escaped from this prison only a couple of months ago. Apparently, these humans had no idea how they escaped and spent days checking the wire fence for weaknesses."

"How do you know they got away, Nina? You've only been here a couple of weeks yourself."

"Oh, I see! You're very quick for a young dog, you know Poppy, but you're right to question everything. Well, on my first day, I was told by another dog. That's the way it works here. News is passed on. I even heard that there are feral dogs in the forest."

This revelation delighted Poppy because it meant that escape was a real possibility, and the fact that these dogs had not been seen since, potentially signalled a successful outcome. She looked back at the pure white husky, who looked confident and very strong. Poppy was well aware that the ability to fight might be very useful in any escape attempt and possible fracas. Even though the smaller dog thought Nina to be aloof and something of a loner, Poppy liked her and felt sure she would be an asset.

At that moment, she noticed the Dobermans taking an interest in their conversation, so she moved away quickly towards the perimeter fence in the hope of avoiding any confrontation.

Once Poppy had found a quiet spot, her thoughts focused on escape and the possibility that she might be able to return home to her family. She pictured the scene in her mind and, for a few moments, revelled in it. Her daydream didn't last long, though, because Poppy recognised the need to be realistic in her expectations. If she was correct, time was ebbing away and, if she was serious about breaking out, she had to think fast and get busy learning the prison routine from the other captive dogs. She had to keep her eyes and ears constantly open and find that cat. A plan was required that needed to be successful at the first attempt.

Back in the van, Bernie and Dave had just delivered the three golden retrievers to one of Grey's regular clients. This man was in the dog breeding business and lived some twenty-five miles from the compound on a remote smallholding. After transacting their business, the two men were off duty and chose to have a drink at the village pub.

Just as they stepped out of the van, a stranger approached them. "It's Bernie, isn't it?"

"Who's asking?" Bernie replied suspiciously.

The stranger didn't reply but just smashed his fist into Bernie's face dropping him to the pavement. Dave was shocked but quick to react, facing up to Bernie's assailant, fists raised.

"Don't be stupid, son. I've got no argument with you. Bernie's had the slap he deserved, and as far as I'm concerned, that's that. I didn't break anything. He'll have a sore head for a couple of days but look on the bright side, Dave. He's still got a job, and at the end of the week, he'll get his wages as usual. Let's just leave it there then, yes?"

Surprised that the stranger knew his name, Dave studied him carefully. He was in his fifties but looked in shape and exuded great confidence. He seemed untroubled by Dave's physique and was not backing down. Dave nodded in agreement.

"Okay," continued the stranger, "then it's goodnight to both of you."

With that, Frank Wilson simply walked away, leaving Dave to pick Bernie up and get him back into the vehicle.

Chapter Eight

Preparing the Ground

After her brief conversation with the husky, Poppy heeded Nina's advice and made her way over to the two young animals standing together at the far end of the compound. Flora was an attractive French bulldog, totally white in colour and having a stocky, compact frame. Millie was an unusually petite Shih Tzu with light brown curly fur. Both small dogs looked friendly and displayed quiet self-assurance. Nevertheless, Poppy sensed that this apparent confidence masked a deep anxiety made worse by their uncertain future. She introduced herself, eager to learn much more about the compound and the humans responsible for their kidnap. Sadly, both dogs had only arrived a few days before and could tell her very little. It was clear to Poppy, however, that they had been traumatised by their capture and were not happy talking about it. Feeling a little disappointed, she was ready to move on but had one last question.

"Incidentally, have either of you seen a strange cat hanging about the place?"

"Funny you should say that," Flora answered, "because we both saw a cat only the other day but didn't think anything of it. After all, Poppy, a solitary feline isn't really unusual in a place like this even though this one looked a little odd."

"Odd?" Poppy enquired. "Why did you think that this cat looked odd, Flora?"

"Because it had dark brown fur and very striking green eyes. Neither of us had ever seen a cat quite like it."

"Neither had I until yesterday," replied the Lhasa apso, "so keep your eyes open, both of you. This particular cat might be extremely useful to us."

Having learned next to nothing from the conversation, Poppy moved away from the two young dogs and walked alone, down towards the wire fence. One of the Doberman brothers followed her and chose that moment to give her a warning. The young Lhasa supposed it was because she had only recently been released into the compound, and he wanted to mark her card.

"I hope you're not up to something, little dog." It was Luther, the more dominant of the two guards. Up close, he looked extremely strong and very mean. "If you are," Luther continued, "think again. Don't be foolish. Only grief lies ahead if you venture down that particular road." He paused momentarily and then adopted a much more amicable tone. "On the other hand, little one, if you are well behaved and let us know what the Great Dane is thinking, your stay here would suddenly become a lot easier."

Poppy was smart and fully understood Luther's meaning, but she just nodded meekly and feigned ignorance. Luther looked exasperated and shook his head but chose not to push it any further and seemed satisfied that Poppy was not going to be a problem. For now, she had to behave like a model prisoner and show the right amount of respect to these pompous bullies. Of course, after her chat with Nina, she knew that escape was actually possible because some dogs had already fled this dreadful place — although she had no idea how this had been achieved. According to the husky, it seemed that the humans didn't know either.

Luther returned to his brother, smugly confident that his warning had done the trick. Both guardians now felt certain that the only dog capable of making their lives difficult was Brutus. He was a firebrand and needed to be stamped on hard.

Once Luther was out of sight, Poppy continued her walk to the fence, where she sat alone looking out over the fields. The wind had become a little stronger in the last few moments prompting her to seek shelter elsewhere but, as she was about to stand up, a movement in the long grass just outside the fence caught her eye. She focused all her attention on what she had seen and found herself looking directly at the aforementioned cat, sitting only feet away from her. Poppy was amazed, failing to comprehend how this animal had got so close to her without her senses kicking in. The grass outside the compound provided excellent cover as the cat moved closer still, remaining out of sight to everyone but Poppy.

As soon as the two animals were face to face, this impressive looking feline introduced herself to Poppy politely and with confidence.

"Little dog. Please listen to me carefully and don't interrupt because time is short. First, I must introduce myself. My name is Charmaine, and I have friends in the forest who are going to break you out of this evil place very soon. I believe it is vital that we all act speedily."

Poppy was impressed. This cat had given her message clearly and in a way that had displayed no fear and absolutely no doubt about the outcome. Unfortunately, the little dog's pride had been hurt by the ease with which this moggie had successfully avoided detection, not to mention her overbearing attitude. She was embarrassed that Charmaine had managed to sneak up on her so very easily and then ordered her to be quiet before their conversation had even begun. So, in a sudden and unwarranted display of petulance, Poppy responded and did so with very little charm and a great deal of sarcasm.

"Brilliant. So what sort of cat are you, Charmaine, that you talk to a dog in that rude and high-handed manner? A dog needing a cat's help? I don't think so! You should be grateful that I let you speak to me in the first place."

This was appallingly rude, and Poppy knew it. She felt ashamed of herself even as she looked up at the dark brown cat with fiery green eyes who had witnessed her petulance at first hand without so much as a twitch. This had been an offensive rant against another animal who was only trying to help. After all, Poppy had convinced all the other dogs in the compound that this very cat might be crucial to the success of their escape. In her mind, she justified her explosive outburst by blaming Brutus, who disliked and distrusted cats and didn't mind whom he told about it.

Poppy was looking at the ground but raised her eyes slowly. Charmaine's face displayed a cold fury, but she remained in control of her emotions. She stood up slowly, pressing her face against the wire fence that separated the two animals, her head within inches of Poppy's face. It was very threatening. Then she spoke in a strained whisper.

"Little dog. Little dog. I am a Havana Brown, a queen of cats. I deserve better. You cannot escape without help, and I am here to offer you that help. You are headstrong, and so I will overlook your rudeness to me on this one occasion, but I will never do so again. Please hear me out and then do exactly what I say. If you choose not to, then so be it, but you will never be free!"

Charmaine possessed charisma in abundance and had an air of authority about her which Poppy, reluctantly, found herself unable to resist. As this remarkable animal continued to talk, Poppy could not help but behave like a small puppy, very obedient and nodding in agreement at regular intervals. A lesson had been learned, and the young dog did not intend to make the same mistake twice. Charmaine continued to talk.

"Tonight, I am sending a friend to speak to you. Listen to him very carefully if you wish to be free. He will help you. Meanwhile, when it is safe to do so, brief your friends about what you have been told and let them know they have support on the outside. You must all stay away from the two Dobermans and avoid, where possible, any discussions between yourselves when they are nearby. None of you can afford to underestimate these dogs because both are very good at what they do."

There was a short period of silence before Charmaine looked directly into Poppy's eyes.

"Do you understand me now?" Charmaine emphasised the last word.

Still feeling guilty about her earlier outburst, Poppy had been staring at the ground, seemingly unable to make eye contact with her new ally, but she nodded meekly, even though it ran counter to her canine nature.

After the conversation ended, Charmaine slipped silently away. Poppy immediately committed to memory what she had been told. To the young Lhasa, any thought of escape lifted her spirits because it was simultaneously exciting and terrifying. She was an unusually clever dog, however, and more than capable of following a few simple instructions. Brutus would worry, of course, but that was only natural for him. Poppy wondered what the Great Dane would make of Charmaine and how he would react when the two of them crossed paths.

While Poppy was mulling things over, a very important meeting was taking place in the forest clearing, only a stone's throw away from the compound fence. A dark brown cat was sitting face to face with a very attentive dog. Instructions had been delivered to the Lhasa apso, and stage one of the plan was about to be implemented. It would happen that night. After the conversation concluded, Charmaine withdrew into the shadows, but the dog remained, deep in thought and looking from side to side in the late afternoon sunshine. Apart from a few grey whiskers on his muzzle, his fur was totally black.

The sound of Jean's voice calling the dogs back to the centre of the compound disturbed Poppy's deliberations and brought her back to full alert. As Jean walked towards the large barn, they all fell into line behind her, very obediently. Once all the dogs were settled in the barn, she left, closing the door behind her.

Poppy suddenly realised that none of them had been tethered, leaving them free to wander about within the confines of the barn. She studied her surroundings and spotted a number of straw beds, most of which were unoccupied. Nina and the other two took their usual places, leaving Poppy to select her own. Not being too friendly with any of them, she took her place on the opposite side to her fellow captives. For the next hour, she made no attempt to talk, thinking only of the worried expression on Jean's face during breakfast earlier in the day. Poppy didn't need to understand the words. There was a malevolent atmosphere in this place, and she now felt strongly that Jean was aware of it too. Perhaps Brutus was still on his own in that horrible shed. She needed to speak to him and asked the Shih Tzu if there was any way of getting a message to him.

Unhappily, Millie couldn't help, and neither could any of the other dogs. Just as Poppy was about to accept defeat, however, there was a creaking noise at the far end of the barn. All the dogs looked on in amazement as one of the boards comprising the rear panel moved sideways and a head popped into the gap. Poppy was the first to react and trotted over to greet the new arrival.

"Hello," said the stranger cheerfully. "You must be Poppy. I've already heard a lot about you from Charmaine." He chuckled as he spoke to her. "I have to say that dogs aren't usually so forthright with

Charmaine. None of us dare! Now then, we don't have a lot of time, so please listen to me very carefully."

The new arrival introduced himself briefly and then told her about the plan. His name was Buddy, and he was a very knowledgeable beagle. His skills included hunting, chasing and making plans which, according to him, he was very good at. Poppy assumed that Charmaine had sent him to assist in the escape, so she listened intently to every single word. Buddy was easy to talk to and raised her spirits by making fun of the humans holding them captive. He even made her laugh a couple of times, which was extraordinary given the circumstances. After a chat lasting no longer than five minutes, Buddy left, and Poppy returned to the others who gathered around her in a loose semi-circle.

This situation was quite surreal, and it took her more than a few minutes to gather her thoughts and start talking. After all, how does one inexperienced Lhasa apso begin to tell a group of imprisoned dogs that a cat is organising their escape?

In the circumstances, even though Poppy herself wasn't totally convinced that a feline could undertake such a venture, she did her best to explain. She would remain in readiness and be the first to go. Once free, she promised to return and release them all. The plan included Brutus, but locked up tight and isolated in the neighbouring shed, he knew nothing about any of this. Suddenly, Poppy had an idea. Buddy, their happy-go-

76

lucky visitor, had spoken of a corridor between the backs of the sheds and the wire fence. Once out of the barn and provided that Brutus was still locked in the small shed, she would be free to wake him and inform him of the plan.

Later that evening, under cover of darkness, Poppy moved the board sideways and slipped silently through the gap. It was deathly quiet behind the barn. Poppy felt sure that Brutus was still incarcerated in the adjacent shed and made her way cautiously towards it. She crouched down at the rear of the structure and barked quietly to get his attention. After a brief interval, she heard the metallic sound of a chain as Brutus moved closer towards the panel. Then, after organising her thoughts, Poppy took a deep breath and confidently ran through the afternoon's events, beginning with the mysterious cat and ending with the clever beagle. Brutus, in his rather supercilious way, argued against it. He reiterated that he didn't trust cats and told her that it would all end in tears.

Nonetheless, Poppy was adamant and informed Brutus that she was determined to escape with Buddy. Once free, she could assist Charmaine by joining her group and breaking all the other captives out of the compound. She also emphasised to Brutus that the escape would include the most cantankerous Great Dane she had ever known. Inside the shed, unseen by

Poppy, the huge dog shrugged his broad shoulders while managing to look hurt and contemptuous at the same time.

After her catch-up with Brutus, it was time to retrace her steps and prepare for the escape. Poppy squeezed through the small space in the back wall, returned the board to its original position and lay down on her straw bed. She had fulfilled all her tasks, and it was now up to Charmaine and her smart new friend Buddy to rescue her.

Chapter Nine

The Forest Dogs

It was almost midnight when, for the second time, Buddy the ever-resourceful beagle poked his head through the small gap in the shed wall.

"Time to go, Poppy," he declared before looking around anxiously. Earlier, he had seen Lester and Luther on the prowl, which had made him feel very uneasy. The two guard dogs patrolled the compound fence at regular intervals during the night and were always on the lookout.

Poppy was trembling with fear but ready to leave and followed Buddy out of the shed and into the long grass just inside the wire fence.

"Stay close to me, Poppy," he told her, "and do exactly what I do because, if we are seen, the humans will come after us, and that would endanger you, me and all of my friends in the forest. It is very important that we remain hidden."

Poppy did as she was told and followed Buddy out of the shed. They went down a shallow groove in the earth that took them under the fence and out into the field beyond. In all the excitement, she could feel her heart pounding as she stuck to Buddy like glue. If they could reach the forest undetected, she believed they would be safe, at least for a while. Actually, Poppy needn't have worried because, on this occasion, the Doberman brothers were asleep on the job and wouldn't be alerting anybody. Poppy trusted Buddy, sensing the goodness in him even though they had only just met. When this clever beagle explained things, he did it very clearly and didn't mind if she asked lots of questions. Her respect for him increased as she recognised how capable and well-organised he was.

In Poppy's opinion, if they had run across the fields in a straight line, it would have taken less time to reach the safety of the trees. However, the beagle's instructions had been clear, and so, whilst still favouring her own method, Poppy chose not to disagree with him.

To ensure the success of his mission, Buddy took his time, moving slowly and stealthily through the hedgerows and long grass which bordered the fields. It was a nerve-racking journey, but the more experienced dog was still insistent that they must not be seen by anyone or anything. It was essential that both animals remained one step ahead of their enemies. Buddy seemed to relish the excitement of it all but remained mindful of the small dog by his side. The journey was particularly challenging for Poppy, who was struggling to keep up, but the ever-patient Buddy recognised that the Lhasa was feeling the pace and, with words of encouragement, managed to raise her spirits.

Finally, the two dogs arrived at a muddy ditch that led them directly into the forest. Poppy experienced a sense of enormous relief when the gnarled and twisted trees just swallowed them up. For a short period, they were safe and stopped for a brief respite.

"Are you alright, Poppy?" Buddy was concerned. "You did really well tonight."

"Are we safe now, Buddy?" Poppy was still anxious and needed reassurance.

"For the time being," Buddy replied. "We have to move on now. My leader needs to talk to you. That's why you were the first to be freed."

Buddy's comments made Poppy feel very special, but she was still struggling to understand why a cat would want to help a group of dogs in this way. Curious but unwilling to ask any more questions, she put that thought to one side and followed him deeper into the forest.

Within a few minutes, they arrived at a small clearing where Poppy felt able to relax and take in the atmosphere of the forest. It was overwhelming for this little dog who was used to a bit of luxury in her life. Now, here she was, out in the open with no food, no shelter and not even a bed to sleep on. Just then, Charmaine emerged from the other side of the glade and greeted Buddy with a nod of her head. After a brief exchange of words, Buddy turned to Poppy and assured her that they were indeed safe. Apparently, Charmaine had been keeping an eye on the compound during the escape and, as yet, it appeared that the Lhasa had not been missed.

Charmaine really was the most remarkable cat Poppy had ever known and very clever too. However, she didn't have any time to think about that because three dogs she hadn't seen before emerged from the trees and stood facing her.

The leading dog had a stocky frame and an intimidating stare that made him appear extremely aggressive. He glared at Poppy and growled, which frightened her a little. Buddy laughed and reassured her that this pugnacious looking beast was not as fearsome as he appeared to be. The brawny looking dog now fixed his gaze on Buddy in an exaggerated expression of annoyance. His name was Billy, and his short white fur contrasted with a scarred face and piercing brown eyes. This powerful animal announced proudly to her that he was a bull terrier. Apparently, he looked after their leader and had done so successfully for a number of years. Although he was friendly enough, he was a dog of few words and always preferred to be in the background. He happily gave way to the second dog, a Chihuahua, who was very much smaller than all the others.

The tiny dog suggested that Poppy call him Charlie because everyone else did, even though that was not his real name. Over the years, Charlie had long since forgotten the name he used to answer to. Poppy immediately took a liking to Charlie because he put her at ease and, like Buddy, even made her laugh, something that she thought she would never do again. After Charlie moved away, Poppy noticed the third dog who had been standing patiently behind the other two. As she turned towards him, he stepped forward quickly and sat down in front of her. The other animals then dispersed, with Charmaine being the first to leave the clearing, closely followed by Billy and his friends. This left the two of them completely alone. It suddenly became obvious to Poppy that Charmaine was not the leader of this group, and nor were any of the others. The charismatic dog sitting facing her right now was clearly in control.

Poppy looked around in the darkness and immersed herself in the atmosphere of this magical place. The forest seemed to be at peace, and she listened as the dense foliage surrounding the clearing rustled quietly in the background. Every now and then, the tranquillity was broken by the piercing sound of a screech owl somewhere in the distance. She studied her new companion's face. There was a confidence about this dog that Poppy couldn't quite comprehend. All her senses were being overwhelmed by the uncertainty of her situation, whereas this dog sat quietly opposite her, seemingly without a care in the world.

"Hello, Poppy." Her new leader smiled at her, and his eyes seemed to sparkle. "You must have a lot of questions to ask me, but it's late, and I have much to tell you. Please bear with me for now. First, I must introduce myself. Everyone calls me Trevor, and I am the leader of this little group of dogs. Well, to be honest, I just look after my friends and try to keep them all safe."

Trevor was a Patterdale terrier and had an aura about him that engendered respect and, by the tone of his softly spoken words, instantly made her feel safe. Poppy looked at Trevor's handsome face and glossy black coat and knew instinctively that this was no ordinary dog.

Safe within the confines of their forest haven, Trevor talked to Poppy about everything from life in the wild to his anger about humans who tear dogs away from their families and then treat them so badly. When Trevor talked, his eyes lit up because he created a little bit of magic that both inspired and energised all the dogs in his company.

Trevor spoke affectionately about all his companions, especially Billy, who had been with him almost from the beginning. Billy was older than Trevor and looked after him, making sure he came to no harm. She supposed that he was a sort of bodyguard. Even Poppy, a Lhasa apso, wouldn't want to tangle with him, and she was a little lion dog. Trevor also described the other dogs in his group, praising their individual skills. For example, Charlie was very good at getting into small spaces, which came in handy every now and then, particularly when food was in short supply. He could also see things clearly even if they were a long way away, which made him a great lookout. Buddy, who had led her to this remote location, was an excellent communicator who loved to dig and was quite the expert when it came to planning escapes. He was also a close ally of Charmaine, the last member of the group to be mentioned.

This feline was extraordinary in her devotion to Trevor but also a loyal and resourceful friend to the others. When Trevor talked about Charmaine, Poppy sensed the strength of their friendship and finally realised why this cat was so important to their overall success. Charmaine was very smart and able to get in and out of places that dogs found impossible to access. The fence that could keep Charmaine out had not yet been invented.

When Trevor finished speaking, Poppy felt humbled by his words and privately conceded that her typically mundane life had not really equipped her to be of any real use to these very intelligent and independent animals. She felt ashamed of her previous behaviour, particularly towards Charmaine, whom she had treated so abysmally. Poppy hoped that she would have the opportunity to redeem herself and help Trevor in any way she could.

After his conversation with Poppy, Trevor called the others back to inform them of his plans. There were now only four stolen dogs left in the compound, and Trevor intended to break them all out before they were moved away. Poppy was eager to help but remained concerned about Brutus because he was being held in a locked shed on his own and was almost certainly shackled. Trevor didn't seem worried about Brutus in the least. He told Poppy that his plans were almost complete and that she would be reunited with her friend very soon but, before that could happen, the possible consequences of her escape had to be discussed. It was likely that the criminal humans would be looking for her as soon as the escape was discovered. Billy thought that they should all stay in the forest, but Trevor overruled him, saying that it would be too dangerous for Poppy and could well be disastrous for them all.

Trevor was adamant and brooked no argument, emphasising that the two Dobermans must not be underestimated. Charmaine wholeheartedly agreed. Perhaps Poppy's escape would not be discovered until the morning, but they had to be prepared for the worst. As soon as the humans discovered that the Lhasa apso was missing, it seemed certain that they would launch an immediate pursuit, even if it was after dark.

Trevor asked Charmaine to return to the compound to provide an early warning should Poppy's absence be discovered sooner than anticipated, even though they all thought this unlikely. The only person who really cared about the dogs was the young woman, and she always left the compound quite early in the evening after arranging their food and water. Hearing talk of food made Poppy feel very hungry because she had been so busy before her rescue that she had not eaten anything. She explained her dilemma to Trevor, who immediately offered her something from his own little store. Unfortunately, Poppy was new to the wild and just couldn't stomach forest food. Trevor was sympathetic.

"Don't worry, Poppy," he said. "I'll sort something out for you in the morning. For now, get plenty of rest. Tomorrow will be an important day."

Chapter Ten

Prepare for the Worst

Poppy was three years old and thought herself to be a reasonably experienced dog. Nothing she had done before, however, had prepared her for the first night living in the wild. With regard to her new companions, the forest provided everything they needed to sustain life. It also gave them a home, a place where they could feel safe and also remain free from the constant threat of wicked humans. Within the trees, the frightening noises and unusual smells all but overwhelmed the little Lhasa, but eventually, she managed to snatch a few hours of much-needed sleep.

First thing the following morning, as he had promised, Trevor escorted Poppy out of the forest and into the countryside beyond. A leaden sky threatened more than a hint of rain as the pair trekked across the fields and over a steep hill before coming upon a number of small cottages that backed onto the meadow. Poppy followed Trevor along a dirt pathway which eventually led to a rusty iron gate opening into a neatly tended garden. In the stillness of the morning, Poppy could hear the shrieking cries of seagulls swooping and diving high above them, a sound which was all too familiar to her. It made her think of home and her parents, but those daydreams were interrupted by the sound of a human voice coming from inside the small garden.

"Is that you, Trevor, and who is that lovely little dog with you?"

An elderly lady shuffled down the gravelled path and opened the gate, allowing the two of them to enter the garden.

"Come for some food, have you?" she said. "And you've brought one of your friends with you. Wait here, and I'll get you both something tasty."

At first, Poppy thought that her mind was playing tricks on her because she felt absolutely sure that this lady had mentioned Trevor by name. She wondered how that was even possible because, to her knowledge, the Patterdale had been living wild for years.

The old lady smiled at both dogs and immediately popped back into her little house, emerging a few moments later with two small bowls, one containing food and the other filled to the brim with tea. She then placed both containers on the grass in front of them. Poppy was famished and wasted no time in starting to eat the food, which proved to be very appetising. The tea tasted rather unusual, but she drank it all the same.

"And who is this little one you've brought to see me this morning?" The old lady continued. "She seems to be very hungry, Trevor."

While Poppy ate, she kept one eye on the Patterdale as he sat quietly beside the lady, occasionally licking her hand. Only when Poppy had finished did Trevor eat some of the food himself.

After the meal, Trevor became ever more anxious, sniffing the air constantly and looking back towards the forest. He glanced over at Poppy, who appeared to be in her element and very comfortable in the company of this kindly woman.

"Poppy, we must go now," Trevor whispered urgently. "Time is not on our side, and we must be ready when the evil ones come looking for you."

He turned towards the lady, bowed his head in a gesture of thanks and then set off for home. Poppy followed obediently.

On the return journey, the small Lhasa asked lots of questions, many of which Trevor deliberately brushed aside, although he did tell her about the village and the people who lived there.

"Don't judge all humans by the wickedness of the men who took you away from your home and treated you so cruelly, Poppy. I have many human friends who will always help me in a crisis and will even give my dogs a safe place to stay if any of them get into difficulty. Without this kindness, I would not have survived in the forest for as long as I have. To prosper out here in the open, you must embrace this life and learn who to trust. You're a very intelligent dog, and you always listen carefully to what I tell you. Discovering how to live free, however, is something that no-one can teach you." Trevor looked right at Poppy and continued, "Nor should anyone try to teach you this."

Poppy stared back at Trevor. Here stood a dog who had lived in a world vastly different from her own. She knew full well that humans were mostly good people because, until meeting her kidnappers, she had never had to deal with the darker side of life. Her parents had loved and protected their little dog, leaving her free to enjoy every single day but, unfortunately, without the knowledge she would need to lead a feral life. She had much to learn and decided, there and then, to persevere with the forest food, regardless of its awful taste. She was full of admiration for her resourceful and capable new friend, who seemed to have an answer for everything and inspired her with his calm demeanour and impressive awareness of the outside world.

"How does the old lady know your name?" Poppy asked Trevor as they tramped back across the fields. "It just doesn't seem possible."

Trevor grinned as he answered, "Well, my inquisitive little friend, it's not quite as mysterious as it seems. My name wasn't always Trevor, you know. Many years ago, when I came upon the village for the first time, one of the ladies I met called me Trevor, and I liked it. In fact, it seemed to suit me so well that I decided to make it my name there and then. After that, it quickly became common knowledge because most of the local people knew each other. Over time, the village became a safe place to be whenever I needed help which was quite often in the early days. Ever since, everyone, human or otherwise, knows me by that name."

Poppy was a curious little dog and pricked up her ears, hoping to hear more. Much to her disappointment, however, Trevor did not elaborate, forcing Poppy to question him further.

"So, Trevor. What was your name before?"

Trevor responded with a weary smile. "You ask far too many questions, Poppy. Let me be absolutely clear on this one thing. I never discuss the life I had as a puppy with anyone. It was not a good time for me, and it evokes too many painful memories. I'd be grateful if you didn't speak to me on this subject again."

Although disappointed by Trevor's response, Poppy had no choice but to comply with his wishes, albeit reluctantly. By the time the two dogs reached the outskirts of the forest, Trevor's mood had darkened; thus, no further words were exchanged between the two companions for the remainder of the journey.

Poppy had quickly sensed the change in Trevor's behaviour and had decided to save any further questions for another time.

Unfortunately, bad news awaited them on their return. Poppy's disappearance had regrettably been discovered, and the kidnappers were preparing to come after her.

"This is going to cause a lot of trouble, Billy," Trevor whispered anxiously. "You must take all the dogs to the old barn right away. I'll stay here with Charmaine and try to throw the hunters off the scent. Together, we'll make sure you all get away safely."

It came as no surprise that no one objected to Trevor's plan, and they all followed Billy out of the forest. To confuse their pursuers, the forest dogs had systems in place to protect themselves from the trackers. Maintaining a disciplined routine and always making use of alternate routes, the bull terrier scurried along a sheltered pathway that ran parallel to a stream flowing through the trees. Halfway to their destination, Billy jumped onto a large rock and then leapt into the water. All the other dogs did the same. Luckily, it was pretty shallow, and even a small dog like Charlie found it relatively easy to move along quite quickly. After a while, they all scrambled onto the riverbank and then struggled up a steep hill.

As they reached the summit, Poppy caught sight of the old barn for the first time, a rather dilapidated wooden structure that would provide them with shelter for the rest of the night. Billy made Poppy feel safe, just as Brutus had done back in the compound. Although he was older than the others and quite intimidating, he nevertheless exuded a kindly warmth. When Billy told the dogs to do something, they obeyed him without question. There was never an argument because he commanded respect, and all the dogs looked up to him. Similarly, Billy respected Trevor and would rarely, if ever, tell him what to do.

Inside the barn, the earthen floor was covered in a sparse layer of dry straw that provided a small measure of comfort. The dogs settled down immediately in an attempt to snatch some sleep before their leader returned.

Charmaine, who arrived at the barn a short while later, promised that she would keep watch for the Doberman brothers, should they have got past Trevor. This was very unsettling news for the fugitives. If the trackers were to outwit Trevor, they might rapidly close in on their position and, clever as Charmaine was, she would be of little use in any physical confrontation with the hunters. Buddy and Charlie seemed worried, which caused Poppy to feel very vulnerable even though Billy did his best to raise their spirits and assure them that Trevor would return safely.

Minutes turned into hours, however, and even the bull terrier was becoming a little anxious by Trevor's continued absence.

Fortunately, these feelings of insecurity were completely allayed when the Patterdale strolled nonchalantly through the open barn door. The dogs were all delighted and relieved to see their leader arrive safely.

"I gave those brothers a run for their money, I can tell you," he said, smiling. "They try so hard, but they're not really all that clever."

Billy sounded genuinely angry when he replied. "You take too many chances, Trevor. One day, one of your plans may go awry, and then we'll all be in trouble. Please take care of yourself."

Trevor laughed and ignored Billy's comments. He just looked around and selected a comfy place to sleep for the night, content in the knowledge that, for the time being at least, all the dogs in his care were safe.

After all the excitement generated by Poppy's successful escape from the compound and the subsequent trek to the old barn, Trevor thought it best to return to the forest at dawn the following day. Nonetheless, he had to be sure it was absolutely safe to do so. Trevor understood that their enemies might still be looking for Poppy, even though he thought it unlikely. Still, he wasn't about to take any unnecessary risks, so he asked Charmaine to return first to assess the situation.

Meanwhile, Poppy pulled some straw over her body for a little extra warmth because the air was particularly cool. That night, as she drifted off to sleep, she thought of Brutus, still imprisoned in the small shed, as well as all the other dogs stolen from their families. These animals were now in imminent danger of being permanently separated from those they loved, leaving them beyond any possible help. And finally, her attention returned to Trevor and the magic he created around them all.

Chapter Eleven

Ovcharka

After what had probably been the most exciting day of her entire life, Poppy settled down for the night within the solid walls of the old barn, blissfully unaware that something very important was happening elsewhere. In atrocious weather and only a few miles away from where the fugitive dogs were resting, a solitary car pulled up outside the gates of a derelict factory situated on the outskirts of a small market town. It was extremely dark as three teenage boys stepped out of the vehicle and scanned their environment cautiously. The factory yard was completely deserted, and the iron gates which should have restricted access to the property were held together by a single rusty padlock. These barriers were unlikely to withstand a determined assault.

Alfie, the gang leader, was clutching a sturdy pair of bolt cutters and a large crowbar he'd borrowed that afternoon from his father's toolbox. The young man used these tools enthusiastically to destroy the padlock, the rusty remnants of which he threw triumphantly into the air. As they dropped to the ground, Alfie's confederates,

Archie and Bradley, promptly kicked both gates open, allowing clear and unobstructed access to the site. Once the intruders were satisfied that no one was going to disturb them, they returned to the car, placed the bolt cutters in the boot and then drove through the gate up to the large steel door of the loading bay.

Once again, they got out of the car and, with torches in hand, moved warily towards the factory.

The main door was locked and seemed to be highly resistant to a forced entry. On further exploration, however, they discovered a small door at the rear which was partially open. Armed with the crowbar and using more than a little brute force, it was not difficult for Alfie to fully open the door and gain access. In their haste to get inside, none of the adolescents had noticed a large gap in the wall where the brickwork had crumbled away. Bradley, the youngest of the trio, remained at the entrance, instructed by his older companions to stay alert and sound a warning should anyone approach from the surrounding area. Once standing inside the structure, both older miscreants felt very pleased with themselves and were more than ready to begin what they hoped would be a lucrative scavenger hunt. At this point, they had already caused substantial damage but considered this to be a necessary consequence of their mission. Alfie's plan was a very simple one. Get in and out quickly without being seen and take anything of value that they were able to carry.

Unwisely, however, believing that any danger would come from outside, the intruders ignored the possibility of a serious threat from within. Completely unaware of a potentially dangerous presence waiting for them in the darkness, the pair moved forward confidently. The beams from their flashlights flickered eerily around the walls, and their footsteps echoed throughout the building. In Alfie's opinion, the longer they remained within these premises, the more likely they were to be caught, and being arrested was not part of the plan. Speed and stealth, therefore, were of the essence.

As the reconnaissance of the environment progressed, Archie made his way towards an office at the rear of the building. Upon hearing a menacing growl, he turned in alarm towards the sound. As he did so, the beam of his torch fell upon a dark shape slumped in the doorway. In this heart-stopping moment, everything changed and the lad's anxiety, fuelled by the constant fear of discovery, transformed in a split second into naked terror. From the shadows, there was an angry snarl, and a large animal rose up and moved steadily towards the boy. Archie was terrified and backed away, believing that he was about to be attacked. As the beast closed in on him, the lad dared not do anything that might provoke it. Whatever this creature was, it was huge, and any thought of a confrontation with this unknown entity made Archie's blood run cold.

Although streetwise and well able to take care of himself, the young man was panic-stricken and, still backing away, urged his friend to run. Again, he played the beam of his torch in the creature's direction and what he saw chilled him to the bone. At first glance, it had the appearance of a predatory bear but, after a second look, he realised that it was a massive dog with a muscular frame and bared teeth. It had jet-black fur, dripping wet from the rain that was pouring through a large hole in the ceiling. Without taking his eyes off the stalker, Archie continued to retreat nervously but finally decided to turn and flee. Both boys were sprinting now, fearing for their lives and screaming out to each other in the confusion of the chase.

Whilst Alfie had no idea what they were running from, the sound of Archie's terrified screams was so compelling that he bolted through the factory door into the yard beyond. Bradley, who had heard the commotion, was already running for his life. He did not stop until he reached the car, opened all the doors and got in. He was closely followed by Alfie and then by Archie, both in a state of panic as they frantically threw themselves inside and slammed the doors.

Safely inside the vehicle, they all breathed a collective sigh of relief. The beast did not follow them across the yard, choosing instead to issue a warning in the form of a nightmarish roar. That was enough for Alfie. He turned the ignition key and, after what seemed like an age, the engine turned over and spluttered into life. In his overwhelming desire to spin the car around and exit the gates as quickly as possible, he accidentally reversed into the wire fence. Correcting his mistake, he hurtled away from the factory at speed. The last things the animal saw were two red lights fading into the distance.

Back in the factory, the Ovcharka growled angrily and then slunk back into the shadows to conceal himself once more. He knew that he would have to move on now. More men would come, and he might have to fight. Strong and fierce as he was, this dog was wise and knew that, in such a confrontation, he could never win. When they came for him in the morning, as he knew they would, he would be gone.

Chapter Twelve

The Dog-Catcher

A sudden noise disturbed Poppy's reverie and, when she raised her head to investigate, she saw that all her new companions were already awake and itching to leave the barn. Reality for these dogs involved a constant struggle and was a world away from the life that Poppy had led until recently. Their continued existence entailed a never-ending battle against both enemies and elements.

Prior to her kidnap, Poppy had no cause to worry about food scarcity or changing weather conditions. In the past, she had been able to take these things for granted. She had a good home and no enemies to speak of, apart from an annoying grey squirrel that she had regularly chased out of her garden and a heron that had often appeared in a tree close to the fishpond.

"Are you ready, Poppy? It's time we weren't here." Billy spoke to her in a gentle way, seeming to understand that she was not used to fending for herself all the time. It was as if he understood her apprehension because he said one more thing before leaving the barn.

"Whatever happens in the days ahead, Poppy, we will all look out for you. From now on, you're one of us."

That simple statement was one of the most comforting things Poppy had ever heard. To be told that she was a member of the pack and would be looked after and cared for meant so much to this small dog.

"Thank you, Billy," Poppy replied. "I won't let you down."

There was a light mist coming off the hills as Trevor led the team back towards home and, hopefully, safety. For Trevor's group, life in the forest was challenging, but it was their home and the place in which they felt safe. Charmaine had departed the previous night with instructions to keep a watch on the forest and surrounding area in case the Dobermans and their handlers were still searching.

On their return journey, some of the dogs hunted for food, small animals mainly, and they drank from the river. Poppy joined them in the consumption, and although this food was not really to the taste of a rather spoiled Lhasa apso used to the good life, she ate it all the same. It was an essential part of survival in the wild, and Poppy was determined to fulfil her role as an independent member of the pack and to do her best not to let the others down.

When they reached the hills overlooking the forest, Trevor stopped and waited for Charmaine to join them.

He didn't need to delay for long because, right on cue, the cat strolled into view.

"They've given up, Trevor." Charmaine appeared to be both amused and cocky. "They just stopped looking. You were right! The Dobermans haven't got a clue. It's safe to go home now."

"Thanks, Charmaine, great work," Trevor replied gratefully. "You've done us proud."

All the dogs were cheered immensely by Charmaine's welcome news, although their celebrations were somewhat muted by the gravity of their situation. Trevor's dogs were battle-hardened veterans, and they all understood that the humans would never give up.

The hunters had searched the whole area thoroughly and appeared to be angry and frustrated by their failure to locate the missing Lhasa apso. Eventually, they had admitted defeat, something they would probably regret when they returned to the compound to face the music.

Generally speaking, the Doberman pinscher is a competent tracker, but Charmaine was right about Luther and Lester. She didn't know if it was poor training or a lack of intelligence, but they appeared to be ineffective guard dogs and even worse trackers. Trevor, however, refused to be complacent about his plan to rescue all the captive dogs, although the incompetence of the Dobermans was a gift that kept on giving. Once again, Trevor thanked Charmaine for all her efforts and promised to talk to her later. After maintaining her vigil throughout the night, the cat was tired and hungry and would seek out one of her human families for a bit of care and attention. Poppy had clashed with Charmaine on their first meeting, but this very accomplished, if sometimes haughty, feline now had her wholehearted respect and admiration.

Safely back at base, within the comforting protection of the trees, the dogs needed to rest. Poppy looked around and chose a comfortable spot adjacent to a large oak tree where she curled up for a nap. Trevor had assured her that he would do all he could to reunite her with her family, but right now, he needed her assistance and support. The life of this little dog was necessarily becoming more demanding and, whilst going home was a distant dream, Brutus and her other friends had to be released from that awful prison.

After a short sleep, Poppy woke up feeling refreshed and far more confident, although, before she could fulfil her promise to Brutus and the others, she had much to do and even more to learn.

Later that day, Trevor took Poppy back to the village for a second time. He told her that she was losing weight and needed something more palatable to her than forest food. He was right because she was incredibly hungry and, while she had eaten some of the forest's foul-tasting nourishment, it was really difficult to enjoy it. She was happy to accompany Trevor once again as he headed across the meadow. He led her up to the back garden of yet another cottage, where he barked twice and stood at the gate waiting. Then they heard a human voice calling out to them.

"Hello, Trevor. I'm so glad you've come to see me again. You'd like some food, I suppose?"

Poppy looked up to see a large lady beaming down at them as she opened the gate and ushered them through. The pair followed the lady up the gravelled path.

"Wait here," she said and disappeared into the house.

Only seconds later, they heard another voice, although this one was not nearly as pleasant.

"Poppy, isn't it?" the stranger said, looking straight at her. Poppy backed away, although the intruder now transferred his attention to Trevor. "And you must be the infamous Patterdale I've heard so much about. Well! You're both coming with me."

In panic, Poppy froze and felt trapped. She felt certain that the repugnant human standing outside the garden gate represented a serious threat to both her and Trevor.

Don Davis was a small-minded and humourless middle-aged man with a chip on his shoulder and no real ambition. His occupation as a council dog warden for the last fifteen years had been unfulfilling and very poorly paid. The man was surly and bitter about his mundane life and equally boring job. He actually hated dogs and could never understand how he had ended up like this. He had no children, and his wife had left him years ago.

Some time back, whilst working on a case involving a missing dog, he came into contact with the Greys at the dog rescue centre. Don was not without intelligence and quickly realised that the couple were into a little bit more than just dog rescue. Armed with this knowledge, he offered his services to the couple in any way they saw fit — for a fee, of course. He was quite happy to supplement his income by doing the odd job for them every now and then. Whilst he would not countenance a serious breach of the law, he did occasionally send the right sort of dogs to the Greys; but was always careful to conceal his part in any of their criminal activities. His latest assignment was to look out for the Patterdale terrier that was making the couple's lives particularly difficult. As usual, Don was more than willing to comply.

As he stepped into the old lady's garden, he quietly closed the gate behind him. Escape seemed impossible for his targets because the fence was too high even for the Patterdale. The human had a van which he had parked close to the cottage gate, and he advanced towards the two dogs with a collar attached to a long pole. Trevor told Poppy to go to the cottage door and wait. He then advanced on the human, watching him carefully as the pole moved from side to side. Suddenly, the lady came rushing out of her door clutching a large poker which she waved in the air.

"Tell me who you are and what business you have in my garden!"

Don looked up, startled.

"Well? Do I have to call the police and have you arrested?"

Poppy could tell the lady meant business, even if she didn't understand her words.

The stranger looked shocked and then stuttered a little. "I am the local dog warden, madam, and I'm here on official business." Don grew more confident as he continued. "Please don't interfere. I am charged with taking these runaways into the council's care."

The lady advanced on the stranger in a threatening sort of way. "These dogs are not runaways. I am taking care of them for a friend. Now remove yourself from my garden before I cause you some serious harm."

Don's newfound courage drained away and, although he protested, his remonstrations were not effective and, muttering angrily under his breath, he turned around and strode back to his van.

"You haven't heard the last of this," he shouted out of the van's window as he accelerated away.

The old lady just said, "Bah."

After all the excitement, the old woman brought out some lovely food, and both dogs sat down to eat. Poppy didn't fully understand what had happened but knew the lady had saved them both, for which she was very grateful.

Trevor didn't say much on the way home, and she thought that perhaps he had become careless on this occasion and almost got trapped. When she broached it with the Patterdale, he just smiled that smile of his and told her about the gap in the fence that he would have used for their escape. Trevor told her that he would never enter a garden that didn't have a second way out, but, on this occasion, he didn't need one because the lady of the house had sorted the dog-catcher out. He then promised to teach his little friend everything he knew whilst always keeping her safe. Later, he told her that the dog-catcher was a friend of the criminals at the compound and must be avoided at all costs.

Trevor looked serious when he said, "That man will not be so foolish again. We need to be better prepared next time."

Chapter Thirteen

A Return to Captivity

Once safely back at base, Trevor hurried off to consult Charmaine while Poppy sought out Buddy and Charlie to provide them with a detailed account of the afternoon's exciting developments. Unfortunately for Poppy, Billy overheard the conversation, particularly the part where Trevor bravely faced down the dog-catcher in the old lady's garden. In his most serious tone, Billy warned her to be especially careful when away from the forest because the whole area was exceptionally dangerous for any dog, let alone one as inexperienced as a young Lhasa apso. The bull terrier then told his story.

"Some years ago, I was attacked by evil humans who gave me a severe beating and then callously threw me into a ditch to die. After surviving the first day, alone and in terrible pain, Trevor found me. In the following weeks, aided by Charlie, he constantly stayed by my side, providing food, water and much-needed care. Looking after me put them both in danger, but they remained resolutely by my side until I had regained my strength. What Trevor did for me all those years ago left me with a debt that could never be repaid. As a result, I became the third member of his little group and vowed to always keep him safe.

"There is, and always will be, an unshakeable bond between us. You must follow my example, Poppy. Trevor is a truly remarkable dog and very smart, but he is not infallible. When I look at you, Poppy, I see a younger version of Trevor, a highly intelligent dog with a clear sense of right and wrong. You must now keep an eye on *him* because, on occasion, Trevor is inclined to behave recklessly."

At the end of the conversation, Billy wandered off on his own, leaving Poppy to digest what she had just been told. She felt privileged that the bull terrier had opened up to her in the way that he had but, despite his flattering comments about her abilities, doubted that she would ever be as clever or resourceful as the Patterdale.

Later that morning, Trevor and Charmaine returned to camp with some devastating news. Following a thorough inspection of the compound, the humans had discovered and fixed the loose board at the back of the barn. They had also found Buddy's escape route under the wire fence. This was a serious setback and completely ruled out any chance of a timely release of the captive dogs. Trevor was sure that the men would now double down on security in an effort to create an escape-proof environment. The proposed breakout would have to be postponed for a while.

Poppy was distraught. To be told that her new friends, held captive by these men, would not now be rescued was a crushing blow. She had promised faithfully that all four of them would be released and was now unable to honour that pledge. Poppy was upset and angry because she knew that these dogs desperately wanted to return to their families, and now there seemed to be no chance of that. In all probability, her friends would be taken away to unknown destinations, and she would never see any of them again. Poppy also had a greater fear. She knew that Brutus would fight the humans every step of the way and that, in turn, they could hurt him very badly.

After she discussed her misgivings with Billy, he assured her that Trevor would find a solution. Unfortunately, time was clearly running short, and this was beginning to seem like a problem that even the smartest of dogs couldn't overcome.

As far as Poppy was concerned, there was only one alternative. Although her choices were stark, she couldn't wait for her leader to devise another plan because there was simply no time. Trevor and the others had risked everything for her, and now it was her turn to take a risk. The little fugitive would allow herself to be recaptured and then organise a new escape from the inside. As far as she was concerned, it was the right thing to do, difficult but not impossible. What Poppy would not contemplate was forsaking Brutus and the others while gaining her own freedom. In the future, this could become a burden that would be impossible for her to bear.

She summoned up her courage and then told Trevor what she intended to do. Predictably, he wouldn't hear of it.

"No, Poppy. It's out of the question. We risked a lot to get you out and don't want to lose you now. Going back to the compound is not the answer and could prove to be really dangerous. You might be hurt badly by these men and then locked away out of reach of all the others. What would be the point of that? Believe me; you will not succeed this time because you haven't thought it through."

Normally, Poppy would have heeded Trevor's advice, but she was a Lhasa apso and remained true to her word. A promise to return had been given, and that was that.

"Do you have an alternate plan, Trevor? One that will ensure we rescue all the dogs quickly? Because, if we don't act now, we'll certainly lose our chance, and I'm not prepared to let that happen."

In an uncharacteristically forthright fashion, Poppy went on to tell Trevor that she was adamant about going back and would not be persuaded otherwise. She would devise a plan to release her friends in the compound and then rely on him to get them home safely.

Although Poppy had known Trevor for only a few days, she trusted him to do everything in his power to help her rescue all the dogs. In spite of the fact that it was against his better judgement, Trevor finally agreed because he could see that Poppy was determined to keep the promise she had made to the dogs still held against their will. Moreover, Trevor recognised the importance of a debt of honour and respected Poppy's commitment to it.

Accordingly, after saying farewell to her forest companions, Poppy followed Trevor out of the forest, across the fields and as close to the metal fence as he dared to take her. The two dogs parted company after exchanging emotional goodbyes, and then Poppy found herself sitting alone in the long grass just outside the compound. She stood up and walked along the outside of the fence, hoping to catch the eye of one of the guard dogs. Trevor had told her to bark loudly at the brothers and then allow herself to be taken inside.

In the event, she didn't have to. Dave was working on the perimeter fence and saw the little Lhasa strolling nonchalantly along the path. In a matter of minutes, Poppy was seized, dragged into the third shed and firmly secured by a leash to the wooden rail. As she lay there in the dirt, trembling with fear, she spoke quietly to herself.

"Well. At least the first phase of my plan is complete! Now I must calm down and think of what comes next."

After what seemed like hours, the door opened, and Jean walked in, accompanied by the cruel lady with grey hair.

"Well, what have we here?" the old lady crowed. "Is life not so good out there then, little Poppy?"

This human had a way of talking that terrified the small dog. A smile crossed Joan's cruel face, displaying her delight at the Lhasa's recapture.

As she spoke, she tapped the top of Poppy's head three times with her bony finger, quite forcefully. It hurt, but as a matter of pride, the small dog refused to show it. Poppy was determined not to allow this evil woman to think that she had any effect on her, neither physical nor mental.

"Sort her out with some food, Jean. This dog is trouble and needs to be sold quickly. I'll work on that later. Meanwhile, keep her isolated."

The lady then strode out of the shed, and Poppy was left alone with Jean.

"Why did you come back, Poppy?" Jean seemed distraught, and her eyes were full of tears. "Surely anything is better than being here. I finish at the end of the week, and I'm never coming back. I don't understand it. You were free!"

Once again, Poppy couldn't make out all of Jean's words but picked up the heavy emotion in her voice which made her suspect that Jean might not be around for very much longer. When the little dog looked up, she noticed the tears running down Jean's cheeks. It was then that the futility of her situation hit her the hardest because she realised that all the bravado in the world wouldn't get her out of this place a second time. The humans would be watching her constantly because she had escaped before. Lying on the filthy floor, Poppy thought about what she had lost by ignoring Trevor's advice and being so arrogant about her chances of success. The fight was just draining away from her, and she felt overwhelmed by her foolishness.

Then Jean whispered something in her ear that changed everything. "Brutus is still here in the other shed, you know, Poppy."

Just the mention of the Great Dane's name was enough to change her mood from dark despondency to absolute joy. It confirmed that her friend was still here in the compound. All Poppy had to do was find him and he would help her.

"You didn't have to come back, Poppy, did you? I think you only did it because your friends are still here. You are very loyal, but I don't know what else I can do for you."

As Jean stood at the shed door, she noticed that Dave had secured the little dog on a short leash, out of reach of her food and water. This was unacceptable, and so she released Poppy from all restraint and left her completely unshackled. Immediately afterwards, to the young lady's amazement, Poppy turned her little face towards her and placed her front paw on Jean's arm, gently moving it up and down. Poppy then picked up the discarded leash in her mouth. She needed Jean to take her out in the open, but the young woman just sighed and left the shed, closing the door after her. All that had happened during the day suddenly caught up with Poppy, and she just fell into a deep sleep.

Chapter Fourteen

In Need of a Miracle

After her conversation with Poppy, a tearful Jean emerged from the small shed and made her way towards the compound fence where she could think about the perplexing and disturbing events she had just witnessed. Earlier that same afternoon, Poppy, the missing Lhasa apso, had calmly and deliberately walked up to the main gate after almost two days of freedom. It seemed as if she wanted to return to captivity because the small dog had made no attempt to run away even when Dave rushed out of the gate to secure her. Normally, Jean would not have been surprised. To a domestic animal, the outside world could be a frightening place, but, for some reason, she refused to accept that the dog's reappearance had anything to do with fear or inexperience. In essence, Poppy appeared to have returned of her own free will after escaping captivity only a couple of days before.

The fact that one of the dogs had absconded caused a flurry of activity at the house, including the dispatch of a small search party to the forest with instructions to find the culprit. In addition to the search, the Greys had undertaken a thorough examination of the compound grounds in an attempt to establish how Poppy had managed to escape without being detected. It took Dave some time to find a well-disguised shallow groove under the wire fence, which eventually led him back to the loose panel at the rear of the large barn.

Since Poppy's recapture, Jean had thought of little else but this engaging little dog. The Lhasa apso had escaped Grey's clutches, not only by getting free, but also by evading Dave, Bernie and the two guard dogs. To Jean, there had been absolutely no reason for Poppy to return. The dog was showing no signs of injury or illness and did not seem to be distressed. This led the young woman to the only logical yet extraordinary conclusion; that Poppy had planned the whole thing. Jean pondered on whether the discovery of the escape route and Poppy's reappearance hours later were somehow connected. If so, then Poppy may well need her help.

Still musing over these events, Jean recalled something her grandmother had told her about an extremely intelligent feral dog that was apparently living in the forest. The locals had befriended this animal and even named him Trevor, always ensuring that there was food available if and when he required it. On occasion, according to her gran, he would bring other dogs to the village, sometimes for food and sometimes for a bit of care and attention. It seemed to Jean that the people of the village had, to all intents and purposes, adopted Trevor. Could it be that Poppy had actually met this dog and that he was responsible for her actions? Jean dismissed this notion immediately and chided herself for being so foolish. Nevertheless, she was determined to solve this conundrum and be ready to help in any way that she could. For that reason, Jean waited until it was dark and then returned to the shed.

The young woman remained very quiet as she clipped on Poppy's lead and walked the young dog through the open door into the yard outside. Poppy was elated but puzzled. Had this young woman really understood her earlier?

"Go ahead, Poppy," Jean whispered. "You lead; I'll follow."

Poppy was excited but remained realistic about the need to take things one step at a time if her hastily conceived plan was to succeed. She made her way carefully towards the main gate and immediately became aware that Jean was not holding her back. Poppy was starting to believe that escape was actually possible when, without warning, a figure emerged from the shadows and stood directly in front of them. It was the human, Bernie. In the moonlight, the man looked particularly ugly, the grimace on his lined face revealing his yellow, crooked teeth.

"What's going on, Jeannie? You should have left half an hour ago. You know the rules. No dogs outside after eight o'clock."

Bernie looked and sounded quite menacing, and Poppy bravely stood in front of the girl to protect her. She needn't have worried, however, because Jean was pretty fearsome herself.

"Bernie French! This little dog has been left tied to the floor on a short lead since Dave put her back in the shed hours ago. Her water was actually out of her reach. You should both be ashamed of yourselves for the way you treat the dogs here. I've a good mind to tell Mr Grey about this. All I have done is given Poppy a little extra food and water and a short walk to the gate and back. Is that alright with you, Bernie?"

Again, Poppy didn't completely understand but thought that Jean was magnificent in the way she stood up to the horrible brute. Bernie muttered something to himself and then sloped off without another word. He remained watching them from the shadows. Jean bent down close to Poppy and spoke to her softly.

"Come on now, Poppy. Show me why you wanted to be out here and what I can do to help you."

Poppy looked at Jean for a few seconds, then turned and made her way towards the main gate.

Jean was very cautious. "Be careful, Pops. Bernie is still watching us, so be quick."

Jean realised that this situation was fraught with both difficulty and danger. What Poppy really needed was an open gate — but not now. Definitely not now. It had to be tomorrow but finding a way to convey that message to Jean presented a thorny problem. In the end, though, the young woman's intelligence and experience with animals simplified the problem. The young woman surmised that Poppy wanted the gate to be opened but recognised that the timing had to be worked out.

"If I unlock the gate for you now, you will be caught in minutes, Poppy. Surely you don't want that?"

Jean then pulled out a small rusty key from her coat pocket and, shielding her actions from the watching Bernie, pushed it surreptitiously into the padlock. She was about to open the gate. This would spell disaster and had to be stopped. Poppy turned and walked away from Jean, growling softly. The young woman caught on immediately and quietly withdrew the key from the lock, slipping it back into her pocket.

"Not tonight then, Poppy. But when? How about tomorrow night?" Poppy was familiar with just one word. Tomorrow! Her parents used that word a lot.

She looked at Jean and barked once, very enthusiastically. Jean then repeated her question, and Poppy responded in the same way.

"You really are a remarkable dog, Poppy," Jean said softly. "I know exactly what you want now."

Later that night and sometime after Jean had said her goodbyes, Poppy's thoughts returned to her sketchy plan. The shed door was closed, and she was alone again and, for the second time, unsecured and free to roam. It was a time of mixed emotions for the dog as she questioned her limited abilities. Was this all beyond her? Would her intervention make life worse for the others? Would she even be able to speak to them? Poppy didn't have the answers but persuaded herself that breaking out was the most sensible thing to do. Anything else implied acceptance of an uncertain and unwelcome future for all five dogs remaining in captivity. Doing nothing was unthinkable, but there would be plenty of time to go through her strategy in the morning.

After all the excitement, this little dog suddenly felt really weary. Sleep came easily as she flopped down onto her little straw bed.

Startled by a scraping noise, the small dog woke up suddenly. How long had she been asleep? Poppy had no idea, but there was the sound of movement at the back of the shed. At first, she could only just discern a shape moving toward her, but on straining her eyes in the dark, she recognised the familiar features of Charmaine as she emerged from the shadows. Poppy was not surprised to hear herself growling. After all, she is a dog, and dogs do not like animals sneaking up on them, but the moment passed, and Charmaine sat down quietly in front of her. Poppy was shocked because the only opening in the shed wall seemed exceptionally narrow and certainly too tight even for a small dog. How did this cat get through it? Charmaine immediately noticed Poppy's quizzical expression.

"I have skills, Poppy. Now, Trevor needs to know the plan," Charmaine spoke quietly but insistently, "and he is demanding that all the imprisoned dogs must be included."

Poppy had to remain confident even though there wasn't more than a glimmer of a plan at present, only the nucleus of an idea. Despite the fact that doubt and uncertainty were her ever-present companions, she recognised the need to stay focused.

"Tell Trevor that all five of us will be coming through the main gate after dark tomorrow night and will need help to get away." She attempted to speak with confidence, but there was a quiver in her voice.

To her credit, Charmaine pretended not to notice. She looked Poppy straight in the eye. "Trevor will be there, Poppy." And with that, she left.

Shortly afterwards, Poppy heard loud, aggressive barking and looked through a tiny gap in the door toward the sound. It was the Doberman brothers, Lester and Luther, clearly visible in the moonlight, looking extremely agitated on the far side of the yard. She looked again and could hardly believe her eyes. Charmaine was standing defiantly on the roof of the house, tormenting the two guard dogs by hissing and spitting at them. What was she doing? Why would any animal do that? They were on the verge of the biggest escape ever, and there was Charmaine, risking it all just to provoke two contemptible dogs. Eventually, the cat turned her head towards Poppy's shed, raised her tail in a thumbs-up gesture and then vanished into the darkness.

Poppy looked across at the small shed that might be home to Brutus and imagined his reaction to the cat's antics. In her mind's eye, she pictured him shaking his head in disbelief. As her thoughts returned to the enormity of the task before her, anxiety again descended on her like a cloud, and this little schemer found herself trembling with fear. For the first time in her life, she realised that the future of four dogs, imprisoned in this horrible place, was completely in her hands.

Chapter Fifteen

Coming Together

Fear of failure and constant, nagging anxiety about the forthcoming escape kept Poppy awake for most of the night. What sleep she did manage to snatch was fitful and denied her the rest she so desperately needed. She rose early, still feeling the weight of the world upon her narrow shoulders, and realised immediately that there would be no escape that night unless she was allowed to mix freely with the other dogs. For the present, the young Lhasa was confined to this filthy shed which effectively blocked her from any interaction with her friends. Events were not shaping up well. Just then, as if in answer to her concerns, Jean arrived with breakfast.

"Hi, Poppy." She crouched down next to the little dog, tickled her ears and then smiled. "Once you've eaten, I'll take you into the yard with the others."

It didn't take long for Poppy to finish off her breakfast and to look up at the young woman expectantly. Satisfied that Poppy was ready, Jean removed her lead and harness, gave the dog a friendly wink, and then escorted her into the yard. Poppy was absolutely delighted because it gave her the opportunity to talk to fellow inmates about her hastily concocted scheme. She knew what needed to be done and believed that all four of her companions had to be aware of the details and what was expected of them. To Poppy, it seemed that things might finally be heading in the right direction.

Once in the yard, Poppy quickly spotted Flora, the French bulldog, who was sitting on a nearby patch of grass with Millie, the diminutive Shih Tzu. She ambled over and stood in front of them both, taking care not to alert the guard dogs. Flora turned her head as the Lhasa approached and growled anxiously at her younger companion.

Flora's owner had been an elderly lady who had treated the little bulldog like a princess. The result of all this pampering had created a very spoiled dog. Nonetheless, Poppy hoped that neither animal would cause trouble when the time came to break out of the compound. Unfortunately, she suspected that both little dogs were the sort of characters who would rather accept their fate, whatever that might be, than risk causing any trouble. Millie looked up to Flora and would almost certainly side with her.

The Shih Tzu was just two years old and very traumatised by her kidnap, which had taken place in her own home while her parents were out. Both dogs had been distressed by recent events and were unlikely to comply voluntarily with anything that might anger their captors.

Poppy would have been happy to let them remain in captivity because neither would have been of any significant help in an escape attempt. However, Trevor had already insisted that every single dog must be freed, without exception.

"Flora. You too, Millie. I need both of you to listen very carefully. I plan to get you out of this place tonight. We'll all be leaving by the main gate, and when we're outside in the open, help will be at hand."

Poppy didn't really think about tact and diplomacy when outlining the plan to these nervous little animals and, rather naively, just gave it to them straight. By doing so, however, she terrified both.

Flora was the first to speak. "Oh no, Poppy! It's far too dangerous for us. Who knows what could happen? Something could go wrong. No! Millie and I would rather stay here, and that's that."

"Are you being serious, Flora?" Poppy was exasperated but remained calm. "Something has already gone wrong. Staying here is simply not an option because neither one of you has any idea what could happen if you don't leave with me tomorrow night. No! Like it or not, you will be coming." With that, she left them alone and headed towards Nina.

Nina was strong and independent as well as being devoted to her family for whom she would have done anything. In similar circumstances to Millie's kidnap, Nina had also been snatched from her home while alone in the house. This had been risky for the kidnappers but worth it in terms of her value.

This was a fiery animal with a lot of pent up aggression, although she was also proud and aloof. Since her arrival, the husky had not interacted with any of the dogs in the compound. Nonetheless, Poppy believed that this dog would be a tremendous asset should problems be encountered during the escape. As Poppy approached her, Nina looked up, took notice and listened patiently as the Lhasa ran through the details. The husky became very quiet.

"Will it be dangerous, Poppy?"

"Yes, Nina, very dangerous, but we'll have help from my forest friends."

Poppy told Nina about Trevor and his group. She also told her about Charmaine, the feisty feline.

"Count me in, Poppy. What do I have to do?"

"When the time comes, Nina, you will know what to do. Just be ready for the unexpected."

At that moment, Poppy heard a small commotion and turned towards the source of the noise. After a brief scuffle, Brutus was released into the yard and spent a few seconds producing strange half barks and growls. Initially, this drew the unwanted attention of the ever-watchful Luther and prevented Poppy from getting too close to him. Fortunately, Luther quickly lost interest allowing the smaller dog to edge quietly towards Brutus. While pretending to scrape at the ground, Poppy laid out the main elements of the plan to the Great Dane.

"The gate will be open tonight, Brutus. Can you break out of your shed when I call?"

Brutus looked at her, apparently offended that she had even asked him.

"When the time comes, Poppy, I could demolish the whole thing. Don't worry about me. Nothing could keep me in this awful place for a minute longer than necessary. Think no more of it; I'm with you all the way."

"What about your chain, Brutus?" Poppy continued. "If that holds, you won't be going anywhere."

"Stop fretting, Poppy. Just look at this collar round my neck. It feels worn through and very weak. I could have escaped the chain at any time I wanted, but, until now, there was no point." He then strode away on his own to ensure he gave the brothers no reason to be suspicious.

As the dogs' daily exercise session came to an end, Jean returned to take them back into the main shed. As she leant over to attach Poppy's lead, she whispered.

"Don't worry, Pops." She pointed towards the large barn. "I am putting you with the other dogs later this afternoon. Mrs Grey told me not to because she believes you will be a bad influence on them, but I don't care anymore. After tonight, I'll never return to this dreadful place."

Poppy felt elated as Jean led her back into the main shed. This would make the escape so much easier to accomplish. Moreover, Poppy would need help to ensure that Flora and Millie couldn't cause any problems. There was a small gap in the shed door through which Poppy caught sight of Brutus walking towards the smaller structure. Even Jean couldn't risk putting the Great Dane in with the others. When he passed the main shed, he turned towards the door and barked loudly. He guessed she would be watching and was just letting her know that he would be ready.

None of the dogs could settle that night, including Poppy. She looked across at Nina and sensed that the husky felt the same. Then she fixed the two reluctant puppies with her fiercest stare. This was it then. They were ready. The next few hours passed agonisingly slowly, causing all the dogs to become extremely agitated.

To keep herself alert, Poppy kept running through the plan in her mind in an attempt to prepare for what lay ahead.

The previous day, Poppy felt that Jean had understood what she was trying to tell her but now, locked securely in the shed and with Nina and the others dependent on her, she started having serious doubts.

Then she remembered the promise given by Charmaine the previous night. Trevor was going to be at the gate and would help them. The thought of her new friends in the forest strengthened her resolve.

Poppy glanced across the shed and called out to the husky. "It won't be long now, Nina. Try to stay calm; we'll be going soon."

She looked across at Flora and Millie, who were sitting together, both with sullen expressions on their little faces. She hoped that they were not going to make trouble on this, the most significant night of her life. It was especially important as Poppy didn't want to let Trevor down. This precarious situation was stressful for all four apprehensive dogs waiting in the shadows. Surely, it wouldn't be too much longer.

Just then, Nina started to growl. She had heard something outside and stood silently watching the door. They all listened. It was the sound of approaching footsteps. Had the plot been discovered? Was this the end of any escape attempt? The bolt on the door was slowly drawn back as they waited anxiously. Then Jean's face appeared in the darkness.

She whispered to Poppy, "Are you all ready? Because it's time to go."

The atmosphere in the barn was electric as Poppy caught sight of her three companions standing only feet away, all looking very nervous. This was really it. They were about to escape. Poppy trembled a little but hid her fear from the others. She was only a little dog herself, and yet here she was, organising a mass break-out.

After one or two deep breaths, she walked calmly over to Jean and then turned back to the others with confidence. "Let's go, ladies!"

Nina moved forward, but the other two stayed put.

"We're not going, Poppy," whined Flora defiantly. "I did tell you that earlier."

Poppy was furious but realistic. What could she do? If both dogs refused to move, then they must be left behind. There was no time left.

"So be it," she said angrily. "I can't waste any more time on foolish dogs. Come on, Nina. Let's go!"

"Don't wait for me, Poppy," Nina called back. "I'll follow you out in a minute."

Doubt was now beginning to take hold. If Nina had changed her mind and if Brutus couldn't break out of the small shed, then all was lost. It was just her alone. Poppy had no choice but to leave and slipped through the barn door, following Jean to the compound gate, which was already ajar.

Jean hugged her and whispered goodbye. "I can't stay, Poppy. If they catch me helping you, I don't know what they will do to me. Good luck to all of you."

With that, she was gone, leaving Poppy standing at the main gate alone, desperate and terrified. She crouched down in the grass which lined the drive and shivered at the strident sound of a predatory bird flying high above her.

133

Chapter Sixteen

A Fighting Chance

Standing at the open gate, deserted, albeit temporarily, by her companions, Poppy's fur was ruffled by a cool north-easterly breeze. Her confidence and self-belief seemed to drift away into the night air, and her emotions oscillated rapidly between fear and shame. Fear because of apprehension about what was going to happen next, and shame because it was she, and she alone, who had persuaded the others to join her in this apparently foolhardy endeavour. All the evidence seemed to point towards it being a spectacular failure, and now it was time to face the consequences — which came a lot sooner than expected.

Quite unexpectedly, she was startled by an unfriendly growling behind her and, as she whipped her head around, she was confronted by two hostile Dobermans.

Luther, the older and nastier of the two, was the first to speak. "And where do you think you are going, little dog?"

Lester just growled in support of his brother. Up close, they were terrifying.

To make matters even worse, it started to rain, and Poppy could only stand there, dejected and defeated. What had she been thinking to believe that her hastily devised plan could succeed? It had always been a gamble from the very beginning, but she hadn't even got herself out, let alone all the other dogs. She stared up at Luther, who was standing there looking very pleased with himself, waiting for her to answer his question.

"Well?" he snapped.

What could she do in the face of such power? Poppy had no reasonable excuse to be standing in front of an open gate. Just as she was about to grovel to her guards, a dog emerged from the shadows, and a very familiar voice drifted across from the other side of the gate.

"Poppy's with me, actually, Luther."

Poppy's mood was uplifted immediately. It was Trevor and he had come to her aid. Poppy thought he was wonderfully courageous, although inevitably, the brothers were not quite as impressed and rounded on him aggressively.

"Be careful, Trevor," she cried out. "Get away NOW!"

Trevor just laughed. "Poppy. Do you really think that I'm frightened of these two pussy cats?"

Lester was greatly offended and advanced on Trevor, teeth drawn and snarling. Trevor backed off a little but continued to goad the increasingly angry

135

Doberman with insults and innuendo. Poppy couldn't understand why Trevor was acting in such a reckless and irresponsible manner because this was a fight he had no chance of winning. Nonetheless, she was proud of him for facing down one of the most fearsome dogs that Poppy had ever seen. She had always considered herself strong and resourceful, but now, standing in the darkness, alone and unable to defend herself, she felt inadequate and clearly incapable of helping her friend.

That was the lowest point of Poppy's encounter with her canine gaolers, who both appeared to be enjoying themselves immensely. Events, however, took a sudden turn for the better when Nina quietly took her place in front of the gate, standing defiantly to Poppy's right in a splendid show of solidarity. Behind the husky stood two apologetic little puppies, Flora and Millie, although it was difficult to see how they could render any assistance.

"Do you need any help?" Nina asked, speaking to Poppy but glaring at Luther with a look that was both scary and intimidating.

Poppy hadn't really considered the husky to be a fighting dog before, but this one was bold and strong and faced up to her enemies without fear. Luther was looking a little less confident now but remained at his post, determined to block their exit. Lester, still facing Trevor, was furious and spoiling for a fight.

Poppy sensed that Luther was about to attack and backed off a little. She was afraid but was not prepared to desert her friends. She needn't have worried though, because seconds later, there was an enormous crash as the door of the small shed exploded outwards. A huge shape emerged at speed from the shed before the door had even touched the ground. Brutus, enraged and with blood running down his face, looked towards the two sets of combatants. The Great Dane had decided to join the fray and strode over to stand to Poppy's left. She looked at Luther dismissively, feeling a lot more confident now.

"We're going now, Luther," she said quietly. "Please move out of the way."

Poppy could almost hear Luther's brain working, calculating the odds. A Patterdale and a Lhasa. No problem! A Shih Tzu and a little French bulldog. No problem. But that huge beast and the husky? That was a problem!

Instinctively, Poppy recognised what their enemy's next move would be because, in her mind, it was crystal clear. Lester would deal with Trevor first, and then both Dobermans would guard the gate until human help arrived. These two guard dogs were not cowards and would defend the gate for as long as feasible. She tried to warn Trevor, but it was too late. Lester made his move but, to his surprise, as he lunged at the Patterdale, a second dog pounced on him from the side of the gate. It was the most terrifying dog Lester had ever encountered — a muscular body with a badly scarred face. The bull terrier had the element of surprise.

"Oh dear, Lester," Trevor said in a supercilious manner. "You didn't really think that I was on my own, did you?"

And as Billy and Trevor took down Lester, Brutus and Nina attacked Luther. The brothers were beaten before they had a chance to fight. In fact, they quickly decided that retreat was their most sensible course of action. There would be further opportunities to tackle these dogs again in the coming days when the odds were in their favour.

"Come on, all of you," cried Trevor. "The humans are coming!"

Trevor was right. Back in the compound, they could see lights and hear human voices. The would-be escapees all followed Trevor through the gate and back towards the forest and safety. This time, they didn't go the long way, but ran directly across the fields and into the trees. Within the protective embrace of the forest, all the dogs felt safe for the time being.

Poppy raced over to Trevor, elated by their success. She couldn't wait to sit down with him and talk about what had just happened. Trevor was very patient with her and congratulated her on the success of the plan but said that it was far too early to be complacent. All the dogs had to leave the forest immediately and lie low until the danger passed.

"The humans will come for us, Poppy. Make no mistake! We have to go, and it must be right now."

Poppy, fast becoming accustomed to life on the move, joined Trevor and the others as Billy led them through the forest and across the fields to the old barn. It was a place the humans had never found and, for that reason, was considered a suitable hiding place. Of course, Billy took all the usual precautions and a few new ones to ensure that the Dobermans could not easily track them. The route taken led them onto the rocks and across the river before they eventually arrived at the barn, tired and very hungry.

Trevor had asked Charmaine and Charlie to stay behind in the forest to keep an eye on things back at the compound. Charmaine made an excellent scout, and Charlie had outstanding eyesight. Trevor always said that Charlie could see things that most other dogs could not, and he relied on that. Of course, Poppy just hoped they were both safe because she was aware of just how reckless Charmaine could be and was worried about her. Poppy respected this impressive cat and believed that her feelings were reciprocated. Nevertheless, she still remembered Charmaine's foolhardy taunting of the Dobermans just for the fun of it.

As the dogs settled down for the night, Trevor gradually relaxed. They were safe for the time being, and his two scouts, left behind in the forest, would keep him fully informed of any threat to their safety. Trevor calculated that the search would not begin before morning, which should allow the dogs a very well-deserved rest.

Chapter Seventeen

Repercussions

By the time Charles Grey reacted to the mayhem outside his front door, it was too late. Five valuable dogs seemed simply to have strolled out of the main gate, conveniently left open in spite of the presence of his two Doberman pinschers. Joan Grey joined him at the entrance to the property, both of them equally stunned at this extraordinary sequence of events. Charles was furious and wasted no time in summoning his two underlings. Perhaps they would be able to explain how a group of dumb animals had conspired to break out of two sheds and open what should have been a locked gate. A conference in the Greys' expansive kitchen was hastily arranged, and all the concerned parties sat around the table.

Dave Dixon was all for going after the dogs there and then, but Charles rudely interrupted him.

"It's almost midnight, Dave. How do you plan to find 'em in the dark? It's pitch black out there, you know. No! To begin with, you can tell me everything that happened this evening, chapter and verse. For example, I need to know why the only dogs left on the property are that useless pair in the backyard," Grey inhaled sharply and added, "masquerading as guard dogs."

Dave calmly reached for the jug in the middle of the table and poured himself a coffee.

"It wasn't us, boss, and that's a fact," Dave replied angrily. "The gate was locked at eight, and me and Bernie came back into the house together."

"Of course it wasn't you," Charles bit back with cold fury. "That would take a bit of brainpower, which rules the pair of you out straight away. I already know who's responsible. I just asked for your opinion."

Dave shrugged his shoulders and took another sip of his coffee. "Listen, Mr Grey. Five dogs may have escaped from this place, but there were at least seven dogs bolting back across the field. One of the additional dogs looked like the Patterdale, but I didn't get a good look at the other. I'm just saying."

Bernie sat there in silence, glad not to be centre of attention for once.

Charles shook his head and quietly left the room. He was a thinker and strategist, certainly not a man to rush to judgement. Nevertheless, he had worked out that the culprit at the gate must have been Jean, the girl who looked after the dogs and who had told his wife earlier that she was leaving and wouldn't be coming back. Although this betrayal made Charles very angry, Jean would have to wait for retribution. He had more pressing concerns, namely the immediate recapture of all five missing dogs, which were likely to be with those tiresome ferals in the forest. He felt certain that the infamous Patterdale was involved in their escape.

After reflecting on his dilemma for only a few seconds, he picked up the telephone and punched in the number of his old friend, Frank Wilson. The man owed him, and Charles knew just the way Frank could repay him.

When Grey returned to the kitchen, Dave was told to deal with the two Dobermans, a task that he would eagerly fulfil. Nothing made Dave happier than when he was hurting somebody or, in this case, two unfortunate animals.

As he walked into the yard, he recalled Grey's words. "Teach 'em a lesson, Dave. Don't go too far, mind. We'll need 'em again in the morning."

Bernie also had a role to fulfil in this sorry saga. He was dispatched to an address in the neighbouring town, approximately fifteen miles down the road.

"Just knock on the door, Bernie and bring back the dog. Frank's agreed to loan him to me for a couple of days."

Even though Charles Grey had assured Bernie that Frank Wilson had no further quarrel with him, the thought of meeting him again made Bernie feel anxious and more than a little vulnerable. As it happened, and to Bernie's relief, expectation did not match reality. Frank even offered him coffee and a few biscuits. Bernie accepted without hesitation. Common sense suggested that refusing an offer from Frank Wilson might be a very bad idea.

Later, as Bernie was leaving, Frank called out to him, politely but with a hint of menace. "Look after Max, Bernard. If anything happens to my dog, we'll be having words."

Early the following morning, the hurriedly organised search party headed out towards the forest. Dave had control of the two Dobermans on separate leads, leaving Bernie solely responsible for Frank's dog, a rather unusual breed answering to the name of Max.

Once in the forest, this curious dog quickly picked up the scent and led the party deeper into the trees. Nose to the ground and ears gently disturbing the earth, Max was relentless in his pursuit of their quarry. Through the trees, onto the rocks and then down into a fast-flowing stream. Eventually, after the scent had been lost and found several times, they arrived at the far edge of the forest facing a rather steep hill.

"I think I know where the dogs are," Bernie said quietly to Dave. "There's a derelict shack about half a mile away which would be ideal as a short term resting place for a pack of dogs on the run. No need to go over the hill, mate. It's easier to go round the edge. It'll only take us ten minutes."

"Not likely, Bern. Why do you think we're following this dog? Let me enlighten you. It's a tracker, and where it leads, we're going to follow. Let's do it by the book this time, mate. By the book."

Dave wasn't about to take no for an answer, and so they diligently followed Max up the hill. It was warm in the morning sunshine, and both men were sweating with the effort of the climb. They were relieved when they reached the peak and stood for a moment to look around them.

"There it is, Dave. That ramshackle building in the distance." A hint of irritation was detectable in Bernie's voice. "I told you."

When Dave didn't reply, Bernie turned around and glanced at him. That's when he caught sight of the two dogs. Poppy, the missing Lhasa apso, looked as if she'd just seen a ghost but, significantly, standing right next to her, he saw the notorious Patterdale terrier that the Greys were constantly talking about. This was the first time that Bernie had clapped eyes on this dog — the genie now sealed firmly inside the bottle.

Chapter Eighteen

Saved by a Friend

In the morning, protected within the secure walls of the old barn, the rescued dogs woke up and began to engage in whispered conversations with each other. Against their will, Poppy and her friends had been thrown into a nightmare world for which they were totally unprepared.

The charged atmosphere was broken by the sound of Charlie's excited voice as he reported back to Trevor on the latest developments. Although the Chihuahua's news was grim, it was not unexpected.

"The search is on, Trevor," he whispered, "and we're being tracked by another dog and not by the Dobermans. It's a different sort of dog, and so far, it hasn't put a paw wrong. I've never seen anything like it."

Trevor seemed worried. "Can you describe this dog, Charlie?"

Charlie thought for a few moments before he replied. "It's quite a big dog but with long ears and short legs. It keeps its head so low that its ears scrape along the ground."

Billy overheard the conversation and stepped forward.

"It sounds like a bloodhound, Trevor. I've heard about these dogs before and what they are capable of. They can track anyone anywhere, animal or human. If we have a bloodhound on our trail, then we *will* be found."

Trevor was quiet for a moment and then turned back to Charlie. "How long have we got?"

Charlie didn't have time to answer because Charmaine arrived and heard the question.

"Hardly any time at all. You've got to go, Trevor. Now!"

And that is exactly what they did. All of them were still tired and hungry, but no one complained. The more experienced dogs were used to this life, having been hounded by wicked humans for as long as they could remember. It was different, however, for the new arrivals who, with the exception of Brutus, were all anxious and uncertain. The Great Dane suggested to Trevor that they stand and fight. Trevor dismissed this idea immediately but, for once, didn't have a solution to this pressing problem. He had no idea where his charges could go that was safe. If the bloodhound could track them to the old barn, then it could track them anywhere.

While most of the dogs chatted anxiously, Trevor spoke quietly to Billy. The conversation didn't last long because, five minutes later, Trevor gathered the dogs together and outlined his new plan.

In essence, Trevor and Billy would take up position on higher ground to assess the progress of the chase, while Charmaine had instructions to keep all the other dogs on the move until such time that it was safe again.

"I was involved in the escape," Poppy told Trevor very confidently, "so I will be staying with you and Billy. I won't take no for an answer!"

Trevor then astonished Poppy by concurring without argument.

"If Poppy is staying, Trevor," Brutus said loudly, "then so am I. Billy looks after you, and I look after Poppy."

"Okay, Brutus. You win. Just say your goodbyes, and let's get out of here."

And so, the two groups separated.

Trevor waited until Charmaine and the remaining dogs had moved far enough away before he strode off towards the hilltop with Poppy by his side. His primary objective was to reach a position from which he could monitor the progress of the pursuing humans. The Patterdale felt that, by keeping a close watch on the trackers, an opportunity to outwit them might arise.

It was a steep and arduous climb, and Billy and Brutus had fallen behind a little.

Trevor glanced back and shouted, "Come on, you two laggards."

It was clear to Poppy that both fighting dogs had enormous respect for each other, particularly following the escape. Here were two alpha males, powerful in a scrap and fearless. Nevertheless, both held Trevor in high regard, which transformed this small group of dogs into a formidable team. Trevor created an atmosphere of loyalty and trust which made all of them feel invincible. Brutus, a powerful and headstrong Great Dane, had only met Trevor once, at the gate the previous night, but was already obeying him without question.

"Are you okay, Poppy?" Trevor was looking at her with concern.

Poppy was young and very new to a life on the run. She had been cruelly stolen from her home during daylight hours and then imprisoned and degraded in a filthy shed with a number of other unfortunate dogs. As if this wasn't enough torture, she had escaped, allowed herself to be recaptured, and then escaped again although, on the second occasion, taking all her friends with her. This intelligent young dog was now a fugitive and would need to rely on all Trevor's skills to keep her safe. As they climbed, a large grey partridge rose noisily from the nearby hedgerow, briefly distracting the Patterdale.

As the group approached the summit, Poppy was about to respond to Trevor but didn't have the chance because, as they crested the hill, they walked straight into the path of their enemies. It rapidly became clear that the pursuers had made much better progress than Trevor had anticipated. However, even though startled, he stepped forward and confronted his adversaries bravely and with a certain panache.

Bernie was initially shaken when he saw the two dogs unexpectedly approaching him as both groups simultaneously converged on the summit. This unexpected encounter was more than Dave could have hoped for, and he whooped excitedly. Bernie, apprehensive at first, quickly regained his composure and reassured the bloodhound, which seemed to be more than a little nervous at this unforeseen confrontation.

Dave remained calm and supremely confident as he released the Dobermans. He smiled as he did so. "Go, boys." Dave, now cock a hoop, cried out again as Luther and Lester bounded towards Trevor.

The Dobermans had been tracking their quarry for hours and had not expected the absconders to be found this easily. They moved towards Trevor with great relish.

"Hello, boys," Trevor said cheerily. " And what might you two reprobates be doing so far from home?"

"Not so clever, after all, Trevor." Luther was not impressed. He knew that the Patterdale was no physical match for him. Trevor, temporarily shaken by these events, played for time while he calculated a new course of action.

"Just give yourself up, and I won't hurt you," Luther growled. "But if you resist, Trevor, I really don't mind if I have to cause you some pain."

He was enjoying the moment, but Trevor didn't react to these threats. Luther, quite clearly, expected him to run, but Trevor merely stared back defiantly at the bigger dog.

Poppy was terrified but courageously stood her ground in support of Trevor. Dave, now close to them, was holding what looked like a wooden club. Still, Trevor stood his ground and, like a chess player, calmly considered his next move whilst waiting for his other companions to catch up. Just then, Brutus and Billy emerged, striding over the grassy plateau, causing both Dobermans to back off a little. Lester had very good reason to be wary of Billy, having been savaged by the bull terrier at the compound gate the night before. Of course, none of this had any effect on Dave, who deliberately strode towards the Patterdale, weapon in hand.

This man was a formidable opponent, even for Billy, who nevertheless sprinted forward to protect his leader. Meanwhile, Dave raised the weapon intending to strike Trevor, but the dog was too quick and jumped back as the club whistled through the air and missed its target. Unfortunately, the Patterdale was now off balance and easy meat for the pumped-up Dave, who punched him in the side of the head with his free hand. Trevor dropped to the ground, alive but unconscious. Angry now and smelling blood, Dave raised the weapon for a second time. He needed to finish the job but was immediately attacked by the snarling bull terrier. Infuriated, the big man landed a vicious blow to Billy's body which injured this courageous animal and prevented him from taking any further part in the fight. Meanwhile, a few yards away, Brutus had been cornered by the two brothers acting in concert.

Poppy watched events unfold and recognised that they were beaten, but she would not run, choosing instead to stay with her friends and do whatever she could to help them. This included the very foolish notion of attacking Dave even though he had already injured two dogs, perhaps fatally, and would almost certainly kill her if she did not back down. Nonetheless, that is what would have happened had Poppy not noticed Dave staring anxiously ahead. She turned around to see what had captured Dave's attention and almost froze.

Standing not twenty yards from where she stood was the biggest and most ferocious dog she had ever seen, black as night and powerfully built. This huge beast moved menacingly towards the brothers and stood side by side with Brutus. The Dobermans now had two massive predators to worry about, an angry Great Dane eyeball to eyeball with Luther and a snarling Ovcharka facing Lester. In the end, the brothers took the only option available to them because they wanted to survive. They fled!

The new arrival had changed everything because the resurgent Brutus was now in his element, proudly standing shoulder to shoulder with his new ally. Both dogs now moved in unison and rounded on Dave, who still held the wooden club, but now in a way which suggested that his confidence had deserted him. Dave looked to Bernie for a little support, but the smaller man was already retreating at speed. Although Dave was a hard man, the Ovcharka was a seriously scary dog, especially when supported by the huge Great Dane, both of them fired up and ready for a scrap. In fact, Dave took one last look at the dogs facing him and then fled like the coward he was. Bernie ran too, leaving Max the bewildered bloodhound standing alone and unsupported in the middle of all the carnage.

Billy rose painfully to his feet and limped across to their saviour to thank him, but the black dog waved his thanks away.

"You are hurt, and you have a badly injured companion who needs your help. You should attend to him. I'm glad I was able to help you today, but I have my own problems and must return to them. I hope your friend recovers quickly, but I must be gone."

"Who are you?" Brutus asked. "Can we help you in any way?"

"I doubt it," the Ovcharka replied. "I have lost contact with my friend Milo and need to find him."

He snarled as he spoke about his friend and displayed anger at the mention of his name. Poppy became suspicious that all was not as it seemed.

"Perhaps we could ask our leader." Brutus was trying hard to be helpful. "Trevor is very clever and might have already met your friend. Stay with us until he has recovered."

Poppy interrupted the conversation, unhappy with Brutus for divulging far too much information to a dog who was, effectively, a total stranger. She remained suspicious of this apparent new ally. Clearly, this dog had saved their lives with his intervention and Poppy was embarrassed by the way she felt. Nevertheless, she also sensed great anger when this dog spoke of his supposed friend. Something was not quite right.

"Trevor will not be well enough for a long time." She spoke with authority.

The stranger was losing patience and spoke rudely. "I have no time for this. If you come across my friend, tell him that Dima is looking for him. Otherwise, do nothing except remember my name. Now, I must continue my search alone. Good luck to you all."

With that, Dima strode off, back whence he had come.

Poppy noticed that he limped as he walked, although she was certain that he had not suffered any injury during the confrontation. Poppy looked again, but the huge dog had disappeared from sight.

Chapter Nineteen

The Counter-Attack

As luck would have it, Trevor was not as badly hurt as his friends had feared, and he was ready to travel quite quickly, albeit while nursing a very sore head. As the pack trudged back to their forest home, Brutus told his leader about the fearsome dog and how this massive stranger had saved them all.

"We would've been killed, Trevor, had it not been for Dima. He'd no time for our gratitude because he was searching for his friend, Milo, and wouldn't be delayed. I asked him to wait until you recovered because I thought that if anyone could help him, it would be you, but he wouldn't stay. He was a dog very much on a mission, I think. Do you know Milo, Trevor?"

Trevor was still recovering from his injury but made himself very clear. "Yes, Brutus, I know him very well, but I can't reveal Milo's whereabouts to your so-called saviour because Dima is dangerous and represents a serious threat to us all. Please trust me on this Brutus and forget about this dog. Right now, we must head for home and make plans to move out of the area for a time. It's no longer safe."

After a while, the group caught up with the Dobermans, who were both showing signs of injury since the escape. Trevor suspected they had been punished for failing to prevent the breakout.

"Why are you doing this, Luther?" Despite the pain Trevor was experiencing, he continued his attempts to encourage the Dobermans to join his group. "Haven't you suffered enough at the hands of these corrupt men? They punish you for failure, and yet you are still doing their bidding. They beat and humiliate you, but still you ask for more. Come on. Use your heads and join us in the forest. At least think about it."

Luther momentarily dropped his head and responded. "You're right, Trevor. We both know you're right. The trouble is we're hated by humans and dogs alike."

Lester nodded in agreement but remained silent. Luther continued.

"We have no future but with these humans. They trained us, and they feed us. We expect nothing more."

Trevor growled loudly, showing his exasperation. "That's absolute nonsense, and you know it." He seemed angry now. "Whatever else you do, please don't feel sorry for yourselves. You have intimidated kidnapped dogs and helped these criminals keep them locked up.

You have been cruel to innocent animals even when it wasn't necessary. And yet, we will all forgive you and take you into our group. We need you, Luther. Be smart and help us. You'll regret it if you don't." Trevor turned away and returned to his friends.

The brothers wandered off on their own to talk things through. From an early age, they had both been trained by their human masters as guard dogs. Unfortunately, things hadn't been going too well for them lately. Trevor had been a thorn in their side for some time and had helped many dogs to escape the cruelty of the Greys and their henchmen. It mattered not one whit who had been negligent or complicit in allowing the dogs to escape. Luther and Lester always took the blame. It wasn't fair, and in addition, they were savagely punished after every escape. Both canine custodians recognised that Trevor had been a worthy opponent who had earned their respect. Now, their erstwhile nemesis had given them a way out that had to be considered.

Luther thought about a life free from the brutality of his masters and without the stigma among his species of holding innocent dogs captive.

In the end, it was an easy decision to make, and they both agreed to join Trevor and his expanding pack, even though they were aware of the problems they would need to overcome.

After their short conversation with the Doberman brothers, Trevor and Poppy walked back to Billy and the others. Trevor needed to speak to the bloodhound alone, but before he had a chance to say a word, Poppy screamed out.

"The humans are back, Trevor!"

Trevor turned his head and saw both men striding back in their direction. Dave had been watching all the time and had seen the Ovcharka leave the scene. The humans, eager for revenge, believed that the odds were now very much in their favour.

"Are you going to let a couple of dogs make fools of us, Dave?" Bernie was now goading the bigger man. "Use your club, man. Teach those mangy curs a lesson."

The only obstacle now standing in their way was the Great Dane but, to Dave, it was no contest. All these troublesome dogs were going to suffer. In prison, Dave had acted as Bernie's minder. This had kept the big man very busy because Bernie had a big mouth and was always in trouble with the other inmates. So Dave wasn't going to let Bernie down now. He drew a deep breath and faced the badly injured bull terrier who was struggling to walk but refused to desert Trevor and his other companions.

Dave strutted towards the helpless Billy, slapping the club repeatedly into the palm of his left hand. "Are you looking for some more, you ugly mongrel?" And then, almost screaming. "Come on then! You've come to the right place."

Billy was a fighter but had been weakened by his earlier clash with Dave. He had never dealt with a threat like this and backed off slowly. Dave followed eagerly, recognising that he had the bull terrier at his mercy. Billy looked back at Trevor for help. Was this the time to cut their losses and run?

"Brutus, take care of the ugly one," Trevor shouted. "Billy, come and stand with me." Trevor, dazed and in pain himself, remained calm and in control.

There was a snarl and a brief groan as Brutus knocked Bernie to the ground and, in a demonstration of the Great Dane's absolute superiority, stood over his supine body. Billy turned and hobbled over to stand with Trevor. Seeing Billy retreat, Dave grew in confidence, chuckling to himself as he stepped forward.

"Don't worry, Bernie. Leave it all to me. These mutts are going to be very sorry!" Dave, pumped full of adrenalin, was thinking about the fat bonus the Greys would give him when he returned home with these tiresome animals, dead or alive. He was now in his element, confidently aggressive but completely unaware that Brutus had backed away from the stricken Bernie to take up position on his right. Meanwhile, the Dobermans were quietly closing in behind him. Now Poppy strode forward to join the action but was roughly pushed aside by a very angry and determined Siberian husky who had just arrived on the scene.

"Don't be silly, Poppy. Save your energy for another day," Nina said quietly as she took her place facing Dave.

It was all over. Dave was surrounded. He had no chance to raise his weapon because Luther and Lester attacked him from behind and Brutus and Nina from the sides.

Four powerful dogs working together and one terrified human. Dave crashed down onto his back, placing him at the mercy of his assailants. A snarling Billy limped slowly towards him, revenge uppermost in his mind. Poppy looked on in horror.

"Stand down, Billy!" Trevor's instructions were heard by them all. "There'll be no more violence." He repeated his words very loudly and very clearly. "Stand down now!"

Billy was staring into Dave's face, teeth bared and his eyes blazing with rage. "No, Trevor! Not this time!" Billy lifted his head and looked directly into Dave's terror-filled eyes. His intention was absolutely clear.

Trevor spoke again. "Billy. If you hurt this human badly, they will never stop looking for us. And it won't just be the likes of this miserable pair. There'll be others, and they'll catch us, and then they'll kill us. Please stop. We have enough enemies without adding more."

Billy paused and then, reluctantly, came to his senses. With one final growl, he stepped back, allowing

160

the others to relax their control over Dave. Triumphantly, the dogs watched with contempt as he scrambled to his feet and fled.

After all the excitement, the bloodhound was offered the chance to join the group but very politely declined. A life in the wild would not have suited him. As things settled down and the dogs started to relax, Billy took Max to a quiet space where, with the bull terrier doing most of the talking, a brief conversation took place. Afterwards, the bloodhound quietly waited for Bernie to regain his feet, whereupon Brutus made it clear that their enemies should leave as quickly as possible.

To anyone who witnessed these events, it was clear that the Dobermans had now become members of the pack. Poppy didn't really approve because both had been unnecessarily cruel to her and, consequently, she didn't yet trust either of them. Nonetheless, Trevor was her leader, and he remained confident that the decision he had made was the right one. In these circumstances, that was good enough for her.

At that moment, Charmaine arrived with the remaining dogs. They had all witnessed what had gone on, but the feline had wisely suggested that Buddy and the others wait for an outcome before rejoining the group. When things looked precarious, and Poppy seemed likely to become involved in the fighting, Nina insisted on going to her aid. Charmaine had not objected.

"What happened up on the hill, Trevor?" Poppy had been there but didn't understand. "You let the bloodhound go, and he'll probably track us next time and bring more humans than we can handle. And then there is the question of the Doberman brothers. I mean, can they really be trusted?"

"Poppy. Your plan worked perfectly. You are extremely resourceful, and I trusted you to get the job done. As for the bloodhound, well, he's a very nervous dog and was forced to track us by his owner, who is a friend of the humans in charge of the compound. He won't be tracking us again."

"How can you be so sure? Once he is safely back home, he may have other ideas."

"No, Poppy! I asked Billy to have a word with him. You can trust me when I say he is no longer a threat. On the question of the brothers, I have been outwitting them for a long time now and know them pretty well. Although we have been enemies, we must look at doing things differently from here on. Things have moved on, Poppy, as they always do, and we have to adapt to the changing circumstances. Now go and feed yourself and then get some rest for a while. We have a lot to do in the morning. The old barn was once a safe place for all of us but no longer. The humans will not underestimate us again. They will pursue us in numbers, and we must all be prepared. Our forest home is no longer tenable, so we have to go further afield to be secure again. Now, off you go. You'll need all your energy for what is to come."

Poppy left Trevor and passed Charmaine on the way to her bed.

"Well done, Poppy. You did really well out there."

Poppy stopped to thank her, but Charmaine just waved her away.

"I am tired now, Poppy, and need to rest, but we must speak about the strange dog. Trevor may be in danger."

By the time Poppy had taken in what she had been told, Charmaine had vanished into the trees.

That night Poppy slept really well. In a matter of days, she had learned so much about living in the wild. At home, Poppy didn't really have anything to worry about, but here, she was an important member of a group of free dogs fending for themselves in a hostile environment. She felt so proud.

Chapter Twenty

The Journey Home Begins

In the early hours of the following morning, Trevor was woken by Charlie, who was in an extremely agitated state.

"Trevor, Billy's in a bad way. He's awake and breathing but doesn't seem able to get up. I've tried and tried, but nothing seems to work. Please come and help him because I don't know what to do."

Panicked by Charlie's news, Trevor hurried to where Billy had always slept, a place where he felt safe — between two large rocks in the centre of the main clearing.

"What's going on, Billy?" Trevor could not disguise his concern.

"I'm hurt, Trevor, and it's really bad. There's no way I'll survive this one. My body's broken inside, and I'm in such pain. What's the point of getting up?"

"Billy, listen to me carefully," Trevor responded quietly. "I will not allow you to give in. You must let me help you. Trust me, I know what to do, but you have to get yourself up. You and I must go on a little walk. It'll be worth it, I promise you."

Over the years, Billy had become accustomed to accepting Trevor's advice without question. Although it was physically difficult for him to walk, the severely injured bull terrier struggled to his feet and, with some difficulty, prepared to move. In serious distress and taking it very slowly, Billy followed Trevor out of the forest and down to the village.

It took almost two hours to reach their destination, a journey that would normally have taken less than twenty minutes. Little by little, however, they arrived at a small cottage at the far end of the dirt pathway. The gate lay open, and both dogs stepped inside, although Billy immediately dropped to the ground exhausted and in a great deal of pain. Trevor barked loudly twice.

It was quiet in the garden for a few minutes until suddenly, the front door of the cottage burst open and a young woman ran down the path. As she crouched over Billy, Trevor backed away and stood just outside the open gate, watching and waiting. Jean returned Trevor's gaze, stunned by the sight of this enigmatic Patterdale terrier, standing calmly outside her grandmother's garden, apparently waiting for some sort of response. Although this young woman had never seen either dog, she knew instinctively that she was in the presence of the much-discussed Trevor. It appeared that this extraordinary animal not only knew who she was but also in which of the fifteen cottages she lived. She looked down at the helpless bull terrier and quickly examined him. Jean's expression was grave.

"Please don't worry, Trevor," she called out. "I will take care of your friend. You can trust me to do the very best for him."

Trevor walked back into the garden and bowed his head. After a few seconds, he turned and trotted away, leaving his closest friend in the care of what his keen senses told him was one of the good humans. He didn't look back. As for Jean, she had been entrusted with a very special job, and this would now become her priority. She had been tasked with restoring the health of Trevor's friend, and she could not bear the thought of facing this dog again if she were to fail.

Later, when the other dogs were told about Billy, no one had any idea how Trevor knew Jean, and none of them gave it a second thought. It was just the sort of thing that this extraordinary animal did from time to time.

Back in the forest, Poppy awoke feeling re-energised and immediately made for the forest clearing to join the other dogs. It wasn't long before the vigilant Lhasa apso noticed the absence of Trevor and Billy. She decided to approach Charlie to find out more, but the little Chihuahua just waved her away, seemingly reluctant to talk to her. In the circumstances, Poppy decided not to press the matter any further for the time being.

By the time Trevor returned, all the dogs were milling around aimlessly, talking to each other nervously about what had happened the previous day. After all, five dogs had just been broken out of the compound, which had caused a lot of fear and uncertainty amongst those released, not least because the criminals had almost recaptured them — twice. On two separate occasions, four dogs had been attacked by humans but were subsequently saved by an enormous animal none of them had ever seen before. Later, a second attack was violently repelled because the humans' own dogs turned on their masters and fought with the pack. Clearly, there was a lot to take in. Normally, Billy would have been keeping them in order, but there had been no sign of him since the previous day. On Trevor's instructions, Charlie had not said anything to the others about Billy's absence.

Just before the Patterdale began to speak, Charmaine arrived and spoke briefly and very quietly to Trevor. After this conversation, he spent a short while in silent reflection, a worried expression on his face, before he started speaking.

"To our five new friends, welcome. To the rest of you, well done! We did it! There are no dogs left in captivity, and I'm so proud of you all. Now everyone

167

needs to know what happens next. Yesterday, in an effort to protect us, Billy was hurt badly by the humans pursuing our pack, and we discovered just how angry they have become. This morning I took Billy to a place of safety and to someone who will look after him and restore his health. Make no mistake; these wicked men will be coming for us again and soon. Charmaine has just told me that more of them have arrived at the compound to help our enemies. They intend to catch us and, if they do, we may not survive."

Brutus, feeling worked up and eager to fight, was the first to respond. "Let them come, Trevor! We thrashed them twice, and we can thrash them again."

Trevor cut Brutus off sharply. "Not this time, Brutus. Don't underestimate their power. I have seen this before. These men will search the forest relentlessly until they find us. Believe me when I tell you that your safe return to the compound is not among their objectives."

Poppy was shocked by Trevor's words but suddenly understood. The humans wanted revenge and intended to dispose of Trevor and his pack once and for all. Trevor continued. "Poppy, if they recapture you and Brutus, you'll be sent away like all the other dogs from years gone by. Flora, Millie and Nina too. For my friends and I? Well, who knows what our fate will be?

It was an exceptionally chilling message.

"I have given our situation a lot of thought and believe that there is a way out that will leave us free to live our lives the way we want to."

He then outlined his plan, which was to split the dogs into three separate groups, each with their own task to complete. In total, there were ten dogs, far too big a group to travel together. Humans would be unnerved by a pack of unsupervised dogs wandering around the countryside at will.

The first group, which Trevor himself intended to lead, comprised Poppy, Charlie and Flora. Their objective was to return the French bulldog and the Lhasa apso to their family homes. Charlie was included because he had been involved with Trevor from the beginning, and his keen eyesight might be needed if their mission was to be a success.

Dogs are thought to have an innate ability to find their way home regardless of the distance involved, and Trevor intended to allow both small dogs to use this ability to get there. Neither one was confident that they could actually perform this task, but they would have a really good try. Poppy knew that her home was near the sea and, once on familiar ground, thought it possible that she could find her way.

The second group would be led by Buddy, who, like Trevor, had enormous experience of travelling through the landscape incognito. The beagle also knew that one wrong move could result in mission failure. Obviously, in the light of his injuries, the bull terrier would not be available to help, so Buddy would be alone. His mission was to reunite Nina and Millie with their human families.

Nina would have preferred to go it alone but, like Poppy and Flora, had very little experience of life without the support of her human family. There was a long way to go and, to survive the journey, both Nina and Millie needed to learn about the outside world from a dog used to a feral existence and who understood the challenges they would face on the way. Buddy was that dog.

This left Brutus and the Doberman brothers in the final group. Whilst the others prepared for their journeys, Trevor talked quietly to the remaining three dogs, stressing the importance of their vital assignment.

"You all have to stay together and keep on the move constantly, running when the humans are close, hiding and resting when they are not. Lead them round in circles until they tire of the chase. Make them wish they had never started this endeavour.

"Your task will be dangerous, which means you must never underestimate your enemies because they will catch you if you do. Be successful, and you'll give the rest of us the chance to get away. You must work as a team and do the best you can for each other and for all of us. In due course, Charlie and I will be returning to the forest, and I look forward to seeing you at that time. Just remember that we dare not fail."

170

After the meeting, Charmaine made a second appearance, this time to warn Trevor that the humans were on the move. Leaving the forest became urgent, and it was time to say their goodbyes. Trevor was worried about the others, but he disguised it well and tried to stay focused on what lay ahead. Poppy was sorry to leave Brutus because, if she returned home successfully, it was almost certain that she would never see him again. Brutus felt the same way.

Just before they departed, Charmaine approached Poppy. "Good Luck, Poppy. Look after Trevor for me, and don't worry about Brutus. I'll keep an eye on him for you."

Then, before Poppy had a chance to reply, Trevor called her over for a chat.

"With a bit of luck, we can get to the coast before the humans know we have gone."

Poppy agreed and dared to think of her family and home.

And so the grand adventure began. Poppy and Flora were full of hope but fearful for the future. There remained so many unanswered questions. What if Brutus and his new friends could not confound the humans in pursuit. What if their enemies had another bloodhound like Max and were already on their trail? What would happen to all of the dogs if they were

171

caught? To Poppy, whatever the future held, her companions were now very important to her, and she would do her utmost to protect them. She was confident that Trevor would get them all home and felt a new strength of purpose. After all, Charmaine had faith in her, and so, she must have faith in herself.

Chapter Twenty-One

Trapped

A little over a week had passed since Poppy had been forcibly taken from her home by ruthless criminals for reasons she did not fully understand. Blissfully ignorant of life outside her own protected environment, she had been thrust into a dangerous and frightening world for which she was totally unprepared. During this process, however, she had learned to cope, thanks to Trevor and his friends. With his support, she felt more than capable of taking her place beside him for the first part of her journey to freedom and home.

In the cold morning air and under lightening skies, the four dogs began their long and arduous trek through the trees and thick undergrowth by way of rarely explored forest paths. Trevor led from the front, walking at a brisk pace and keeping their spirits up with gentle words of encouragement.

Before long, the resolute foursome emerged from the trees on the outer edge of the forest. Poppy looked across the unfamiliar terrain and shivered. Standing quietly on the brink of a completely new world, she surveyed the scene carefully. It was clear that the group would have to travel across open ground, in plain sight for much of the time, thereby leaving them vulnerable. Poppy understood the perilous nature of the task before them, one which would demand all of Trevor's special skills to ensure a successful outcome. She imagined that many humans would be out looking for them, but Trevor dismissed the notion with a wave of his paw.

"How many humans do you think will be tracking us, Poppy? If they want to catch us all, they will need a lot of help and quickly. I can't see that there'll be any more than two on our trail."

"I hope you're right," Poppy replied quietly, but she was worried about her leader because he didn't quite seem himself. "Are you alright, Trevor?" she enquired.

"Of course I am, Poppy. Apart from a bad headache, I'm fine. Look, it's good to be cautious, but we have to keep on the move. These humans won't stop, and neither will we."

By remaining tactically one step ahead of their enemies and keeping off the beaten track, Trevor believed that they would be safe. His main concern was the welfare and safety of the dogs in his care. He had, therefore, chosen the less travelled route even though its use entailed a longer journey over more demanding terrain. The Patterdale remained confident of success even though the group now lacked the protection of the stronger members of the pack. His mission was to successfully reunite the two inexperienced dogs with their families, a task that would certainly require the invaluable assistance of Charlie, his close friend, and a dog never to be underestimated. Although it was a daunting endeavour, this remarkable terrier intended to do his absolute best never to fail any of his companions.

By late morning, after travelling a good many miles, the dogs were becoming weary and needed to rest. As the party traversed the fields, the ever-vigilant Chihuahua spotted a small area of meadow, surrounded by trees and a few bushes, where he suggested they rest and plan their next move. Trevor agreed and, while the two cannier dogs explored the territory, Poppy and Flora settled down in the grass to relax. When the two scouts eventually returned, Trevor sat and spoke to both young dogs.

"We've had a good look round, but neither of us can see a clear route to the beach without going through the town," he said quietly. "I'm fully aware you have never been in a town on your own before. In the circumstances, we must wait until it starts getting dark, even though every minute spent hiding increases our risk of capture.

"The two men we encountered on the hill yesterday may well be tracking us by now, so I need you to listen carefully. Humans are suspicious of unsupervised dogs travelling on their own because they become concerned for their own safety. Because of this, it would not be sensible to walk down the street together — at any time of day. So, when the time is right, we will go in twos. Poppy, you will travel with Charlie and do everything he tells you. I'll wait for a while and then follow on with Flora. Now, settle down and rest. We have plenty of time to regain our strength before the sun goes down."

The seriousness of the undertaking in which she was involved was beginning to affect Poppy, and she found it extremely difficult to relax.

When the time came to move, however, even though nervous and anxious, she followed Charlie across the grassy meadow and into the town. The main street which led towards the beach was lined with lofty buildings that loomed above them as they edged forward into the throng of busy people going about their business.

Charlie stood by her side. "This is it, Poppy! Stick to me like glue."

Charlie began to walk down the busy thoroughfare, looking extremely self-assured. Poppy followed. There were lots of people going in and out of the shops and, at first, nobody took any notice of the two little dogs. In fact, they made such good progress that they were halfway down the street before a problem arose.

A couple of humans were taking more than a passing interest in them, and Charlie had to warn Poppy to be careful. She thought it was time to run, but Charlie had other ideas. Calmly and without causing Poppy to panic, he just sat in one of the shop doorways and remained very still. Poppy did the same. Then, as a friendly-looking couple emerged from the store, Charlie followed them, staying very close. Poppy caught on quickly and selected her own humans to walk behind. To the Lhasa, this seemed to be a strategy that would reassure any disconcerted onlookers while creating the illusion of normality. By now, the apparently suspicious humans had lost interest and wandered off without even glancing back.

As soon as Charlie thought it was safe, both dogs continued on their way, trailing different humans whenever they needed to. Charlie remained calm and collected at all times, and this helped Poppy to retain her composure.

As they walked, he spoke to her. "Poppy. If I tell you to run, then you must run."

"Where do I run, Charlie? I'm frightened now, and I'm with you. What will I be like on my own?"

"If and when the time comes, Poppy, you'll know what to do. Otherwise, you are doing just fine."

Luckily they had nothing further to worry about and quickly reached the far end of the street and relative safety. If she tried very hard, she could now make out the shimmering surface of the sea in the distance. This made her feel a little better despite the exhausting nature of the whole episode.

Moments later, Trevor arrived with Flora, who was trembling and appeared to be absolutely terrified. In an effort to calm her down, Trevor just smiled and told her she had done well.

"You too, Poppy. Now we need food because we still have a long way to go. Look after Flora for a little while. Charlie and I will be back very soon."

With that, the pair of them trotted back down the street and vanished into a side alley.

Flora and Poppy didn't have long to wait. Trevor and Charlie were back after only a few minutes, both holding slices of meat in their jaws. In all the excitement, the dogs had put their hunger to one side in their efforts to avoid capture, but the smell of the food was irresistible.

Trevor realised how eager his young companions were to eat and cautioned them. "Not here, Poppy. It's too dangerous. Let's get to a safer place."

Trevor headed for the beach, which was populated by only a handful of people who had been enjoying a stroll along the sands, some exercising their dogs. It was becoming dark, and as they moved forward, two Staffordshire bull terriers approached, one of the pair acting very aggressively.

"Who are you, and what are you doing here?"

"We're no threat to you," Trevor replied amicably. "We are being hunted by humans and need to find a safe place to rest. I am responsible for my three friends here."

The hostile Staffie continued. "That's not our problem, friend. Leave here now and don't return."

Just then, the second Staffie, a smaller but friendlier dog than the first, took an interest in the conversation.

"Please excuse my brother. He likes to act tough, but in reality, he is less dangerous than a kitten. His name is Rufus, and I am Mattie. You are a Patterdale, I think. Might your name be Trevor?"

The question took Trevor completely by surprise. "Yes, Mattie, you are right, but my name is not important right now. My friends and I are in danger, and we need help. Is there anywhere that we might get out of this wind for a while? Somewhere we would be less conspicuous than out here in the open."

Rufus immediately turned towards Trevor and bowed his head submissively. "I am so sorry, Trevor. Dogs talk about your exploits wherever we go, but I never thought that I would meet you. Please forgive me. There are some rocks a little further on which will give you some shelter for a while but don't stay there too long. It's not completely safe."

Rufus was about to explain the reason for his warning when a loud whistle interrupted the conversation, followed by a human voice calling the Staffies away.

"Good luck Trevor," cried Mattie as she bounded across the sand, followed by Rufus. Seconds later, Trevor and the others were alone again.

After this unexpected encounter, the near-exhausted travellers continued along the shore for a while before coming across a small circle of tall jagged rocks. In the centre of this outcrop was an enclosed space where the dogs could rest and take advantage of a little shelter from the wind that was gathering strength. Trevor found a quiet corner, not visible to the humans on the beach, where they settled down to rest.

As Poppy tucked into the food, she looked around anxiously, realising that the group was extremely vulnerable to an attack by their enemies. If this were to happen, they would have nowhere to run. She glanced over at Trevor, who seemed unaware of the precarious nature of their position. They were sitting inside a circle of stones with only one exit.

"I'm thirsty, Trevor. I haven't had a drink for ages," Flora whined.

"None of us have!" Poppy snapped back, her patience at breaking point. "But we aren't complaining, Flora. Be grateful for a change."

The little bulldog scowled back at Poppy but said nothing. Trevor calmly assured Flora that they would all get a drink soon, but first, they had to eat. After that, the group needed to conserve their strength so that, if necessary, they would be physically prepared to move on at a moment's notice. The rocky enclosure provided the four fugitives with a relatively peaceful retreat in which to talk things through, although Poppy's concerns about their insecure position compelled her to take the situation seriously and explore on her own.

From an initial inspection, there appeared to be only one way in and out, which was dangerous if they were cornered. She voiced her concerns to Trevor, but he dismissed them and told her not to worry. There was now no doubt in Poppy's mind that, since the big human had battered the side of Trevor's head, the Patterdale had not seemed himself. Usually, he was meticulous in his attention to detail, particularly when his enemies were around. However, as they lay concealed within the rocks, there was precious little indication of any planning at all.

The night was drawing in fast, and Trevor finally seemed to become aware of the danger. If spotted, they had little chance of escape. Flora, who never wanted to take part in what she thought was a potentially ill-fated venture, was worried too.

"Please. Can we leave this place now, Trevor?"

"Not yet," Trevor replied. "We cannot move until I am sure it is safe. Whilst stealing the food, we were seen. I don't want to alarm you both but two of the humans who saw us were from the compound, and they were not alone. Their companion was another man that you and I have already met, Poppy. You remember, I'm sure, because he tried to take us out of the old lady's garden. We were too quick for them today, but now they know we are here, they've got the means to follow us anywhere we go. They may even get ahead of us to organise a trap."

Just then, Trevor heard a low growling and realised that Charlie was on full alert.

"There's two of them, Trevor, and they're coming this way. And there's another human in the van."

Charlie had remarkable eyesight, but he wasn't a fighter. Poppy wished that Brutus and Billy were here right now.

"Surely we are faster than humans," Poppy said urgently. "Let's make a run for it."

Trevor was quick to respond. "No, Poppy. They are looking for us but don't know exactly where we are. We're all tired and may end up running straight into a trap. Stay quiet, and we'll be safe."

Trevor seemed confident that the humans tracking them would simply pass by, but Poppy wasn't so sure. At first, the humans did walk beyond the rocks, followed closely by the white van, which drove slowly past the outcrop and continued on its way.

Moments later, however, all four dogs heard the sound of men scurrying across the sand, calling out to each other in loud voices as they closed off the exit from the rocky hiding place. This was a catastrophic blow to Trevor, who finally had to accept the uncomfortable truth that, for the first time in his life, he had been well and truly outwitted by humans who had doubled back to the rocks and trapped them inside.

Trevor and Charlie prepared to resist, although both knew it was hopeless. They barked and tried very hard to threaten their enemies, but they had been caught cold. It was as if these men had known the dogs were there all along.

Chapter Twenty-Two

Unexpected Help

Bernie French and volatile muscleman Dave Dixon were in a lot of trouble with their employers, Charles and Joan Grey. Two days ago, five valuable canines had escaped from the compound aided by a pack of troublesome ferals living wild in the nearby forest. Having successfully located the missing animals on a hillside the following morning, the two men had dismally failed to recapture them—twice.

Charles was absolutely furious when told. Had their mission proved successful, the haul might have included the infamous Patterdale and his fellow pack member, the despised bull terrier. His mood deteriorated further still when he learned that, during the first attempt to recapture the runaways, a ferocious canine predator of unknown origin had appeared from nowhere to assist them. Even worse, on the second attempt, Grey's own Doberman pinschers had actively aided the escaped dogs by fighting alongside them. A number of colourful adjectives had been applied to the two men, none of which were complimentary. Nonetheless, they were given one final opportunity to redeem themselves by capturing and returning all the escaped dogs to the compound very speedily. They had also been instructed to show no mercy to any feral dog that got in their way.

In normal circumstances, for Dave and Bernie, this would have been a welcome opportunity to save face. However, sadly, it was conditional upon accepting the assistance of the crooked dog warden, Don Davis, who would be directing the operation. The two men were given no choice other than to tolerate this arrangement — better that than losing their jobs or, worse still, taking a beating.

Evidently, Grey had the utmost faith in the dog warden and sincerely believed that this man could successfully track the dogs to their current location and then recover them all.

The pursuit began in the forest the following morning; on this occasion, without any canine support. Even though Max, the nervous bloodhound, had been returned to his home unharmed, Frank Wilson had refused to offer any further assistance. This threatened to make life very difficult for the trackers, although they had no choice but to proceed with the hunt.

After a cursory examination of the ground, it became clear that the dogs had organised themselves into groups. To counter this strategy, the dog-catcher did the same, one team for each pack of dogs. After an exploratory search, it became clear that two of the groups had set off in opposite directions out of the forest, with the remainder heading further into the trees.

Don was reluctant to chase shadows and so returned to the compound to plan the next phase of this complex operation. He needed to have his wits about him and be organised. The Greys had offered a bonus for every dog returned and an even bigger bonus for the Patterdale, dead or alive.

Although outwardly confident, Don feared the consequences of failure and worried about the huge responsibility placed upon him by Grey. Nonetheless, regardless of his misgivings, he badly wanted to catch this feral dog but had, as yet, no idea which of the three routes it might have taken. This was a problem that needed a rapid and well-considered solution.

Don was desperate to get on the trail of the Patterdale, the pack leader, and the dog that had caused so much aggravation. He unfolded his map for a moment and studied all the routes out of the forest. One, in particular, caught his eye and, as he examined it closely, he first grimaced and then smiled.

The journey to the coast would not be an easy one and would involve going through a town. He became convinced that this would be his quarry's chosen escape route, not only because it was the most challenging option but because the terrain would make it far more difficult for humans to maintain any sort of pursuit. Don chuckled at the simple way his adversary's mind worked.

The dog warden had no intention of following these wretched animals along their favoured route, preferring to move ahead of them and then trap them like fish in a barrel. Feeling confident and in a much lighter mood, he kept his thoughts to himself as he briefed his men.

As soon as all the trackers were fully prepared and had received their instructions, they set about their allotted tasks. Don insisted on taking the van and invited Bernie and his mate, Dave, to join him. He could always use a bit of muscle in the event of any unforeseen problems. The three men left the compound and headed out onto the coast road with Bernie at the wheel of the van.

Naturally, as in all strategies, there was a possibility that Don was wrong, although, despite the risks, he had to remain confident and be prepared to back his own judgement.

"Put your foot down, Bernie. If you can get us into town before those miserable curs, they'll walk right up to us."

Although Bernie didn't like Don, he accepted that the man knew far more about dogs than he did, and so, by doing precisely what he had been told, it wasn't going to be his fault if these animals eluded them yet again.

As a man, Don was weak and ineffectual but, in his role as a dog warden, he had considerable experience of canine behaviour. This special knowledge enabled him to predict how a dog with normal intelligence might react in certain situations.

Unfortunately, the man could not be sure which dogs he was tracking, nor how many, and this placed him in a difficult position. If the Patterdale was indeed leading the group he was pursuing, his job was likely to be far more difficult. In his previous encounter with this dog, he had become aware of its exceptional intelligence, so much so that he had begun to question his own ability to outsmart it.

As the van reached the town, all three men scanned the main street as Bernie parked up outside the local supermarket. It was uncomfortable for three people in the front seat but, just as they began to get irritable, Bernie made the first contact. He spotted the Patterdale and the Chihuahua openly stealing food from a bin between two shops.

Although all three immediately set off in pursuit, the dogs gave them the slip in the busy thoroughfare. Forced to abandon the chase, they returned to the van to consider what to do, confident that the dogs would have already chosen a nearby location where they could settle down for the night.

The dog warden favoured maintaining close contact with their quarry, but Dave wanted sustenance and wouldn't go anywhere until he had eaten and downed one or two beers. Don was terrified of the vicious thug and didn't intend to argue. Instead, he settled for a short break, although it was almost dark when they emerged from the pub and resumed their hunt for the fugitives. The dogs had been caught cold and were now on the run, almost certainly feeling the proximity of their hunters.

Nevertheless, while the three men had been sitting in the pub drinking, the pack leader and his little gang had been given precious time to evade capture.

On the beach, Don looked to his left and then to his right, trying to work out which direction the fugitives had taken. It was so easy to get it wrong, and that is exactly what he did. He turned to the right and wasted another hour before he realised his mistake and turned back. Finally, they were going in the right direction, although darkness had now descended, and this made the task of finding the dogs far more difficult. Bernie drove the van slowly across the smooth sand, keeping behind the other two who were trudging laboriously across the beach, torches in hand.

"That's a likely hiding place, Dave," Don spoke quietly, indicating to a small rocky area immediately to his left. Until now, there had been lots of paw prints in the wet sand but, as they walked beyond the entrance, the surface became even and unmarked.

To avoid playing their hand too early, Don instructed Bernie to continue along the beach while the other two sneaked back, relying on the element of surprise. Once the van moved away, Don threw a net over his shoulder and took a cattle prod out of his jacket pocket.

"They're in the rocks, Dave. I think we've cracked it. Use the grasper, mate. Let's not muck it up this time."

There was a bit of a scuffle as Trevor and Charlie were caught, and then Flora succumbed. At that point, it seemed to be all over because the only dog still at liberty was Poppy, although the villains didn't realise she was there. Don looked upon this operation as a success. After all, he had retrieved one of the escaped dogs, but more importantly, he had captured the notorious Patterdale and another member of his pack. The Greys would have to be pleased with that.

Hiding only a few feet away from her enemies, Poppy was far from safe and knew that the humans would easily find her if she failed to find a way out. The rocks were smooth and slippery and impossible to climb, but as she cowered in a tiny space between two huge boulders, the little dog noticed something that she hadn't spotted before. There was a small opening at the innermost point, which seemed to be just big enough for a small dog to slip through. She thought of the night Charmaine had surprised her in the barn by squeezing through an impossibly small opening. And she remembered Charmaine's words.

She spoke quietly to herself. "Well, dogs have skills too, Charmaine!"

She had just one chance, which happily proved to be effective. The little dog wiggled through the gap and ran. If she was caught, then it really was all over — escape meant that she would, at least, be free to help her friends.

As Poppy raced across the sand, she looked back just once. The van's headlights partially illuminated the scene, and the light from torches flickered haphazardly in the night sky. She lay down in wet sand, very close to the small waves breaking onto the shore. No one followed. No one knew she was there.

Alone and terrified, Poppy watched in horror as her three friends were secured and then bundled into the white van that had become so familiar to her. When Trevor fought back, Poppy saw one of the men touch his hindquarters with a short metal stick and heard her friend yelp in pain. None of her companions stood a chance.

So intently was Poppy watching that she didn't notice three large forms standing behind her until a throaty growl made her aware of their company. She jumped up, ready to run, but the figures weren't human. They were dogs and big ones at that. She should have been more alert, but the wind was quite strong and coming off the land. These strangers had moved downwind of her to ensure she did not catch their scent.

"Come with us, now," uttered one of the new arrivals. "You don't have long!"

"No. My friends have been seized, and I must help them before they're taken away." Poppy was pleading now and very upset.

The dog just growled again. "The humans will not be going anywhere. The sea has already cut them off. The water comes in really fast around here."

It was true. The tide was still coming in steadily, covering much of the sandy beach. The van was safe and parked on a concrete apron close to the rocks, but it would be unable to move because the water had locked it in at both ends of the beach.

Poppy remained concerned for her friends but knew she had no choice but to go with the new arrivals. She followed them along the shore until they came to some concealed steps built into the cliff. All four dogs climbed to the top and settled down in the grass. From this vantage point, Poppy had a clear view of the whole beach, including the van, which was now completely cut off by the sea.

While sitting by the clifftop, she took the opportunity to study her companions, all large, powerful males. They were not as big as Brutus but certainly dogs to be reckoned with. Not only were they strong, but they also exuded confidence.

"What next?" Poppy asked politely.

"We wait," the leader said. "And, while we wait, you can tell us all about yourself and why these humans have been chasing you."

At first, Poppy was guarded and told them very little, but, in the end, she opened up and told them everything about her kidnap, imprisonment and subsequent escape from the compound. She told them her name and the names of all the other dogs in her group. They were particularly interested in Trevor.

After hearing her story, the leader spoke again.

"Little dog, my name is Oscar, and I know all about bad humans. In the past, me and my two friends, Romeo and Victor here, worked for good humans. Our job was to help catch the bad ones."

"I don't understand," Poppy said. "How did you know these other humans were bad?"

Oscar thought for a moment and then smiled. "We all knew that our humans were good people, and this was our yardstick for judging others. That was sufficient for us. Dogs sense things, don't they, Poppy?"

She had to admit it. He was right. She could always tell the good from the bad. It's just a natural talent that dogs possess.

Oscar continued to tell Poppy quite a lot about their work. The three of them hadn't always worked together and had been asked to do lots of different things. Victor, for example, had been trained to find things for humans by sniffing them out and Romeo used to work in places where thousands of humans all gathered together. To Poppy, all three of her new friends seemed very impressive.

"Well, Poppy," growled Oscar, "I am beginning to understand your situation and why you need our help. Come with us."

If this wasn't quite a command, it wasn't a request either. Poppy didn't think it was unkindly meant, and she didn't argue. She just followed Oscar, leaving the other two to follow behind.

After only a few minutes, they arrived at an isolated house standing on one side of a long lane. Poppy was reminded of the remote house in the centre of the compound, but this place was different. She sensed no evil and saw no high fences. The house was surrounded by a low stone wall, although they could access the garden through an open gate. Oscar and the others sauntered through the gap into a small open shed.

Poppy must have looked surprised because Romeo turned to her and said, "Not all places are evil, Poppy."

The shed was nothing like the dilapidated wooden structures at the compound. It felt like a home designed for dogs, complete with comfortable beds and food and drink.

"Help yourself, Poppy," said Romeo. "You must be starving by now. After you have eaten, we'll work out what to do about your situation. Don't worry. We'll rescue your friends. Have no doubt about that."

Poppy settled down, secure in the knowledge that she was safe and in the company of friends. These dogs didn't waste words but, deep down, she felt they had good hearts and excellent intentions. For now, she was tired and, after eating more than she should have, could not resist a snooze.

On the beach, Don and his cronies were jubilant. The infamous Patterdale and two other dogs were safely locked in the van. However, as Don looked across the beach, he was stunned by the speed of the incoming tide, which had completely cut them off. They hadn't noticed, mainly due to their ignorance of the local tides and partly because the area in which the van was parked was slightly raised and had looked completely safe.

"What do we do now, Donald?" Dave asked sarcastically.

"Get in the van, Dave," the dog warden replied. "We've just got to wait. It's a small price to pay considering we got all three dogs, including the Patterdale."

"If it's still alive in the morning, mate." Dave disliked Don and made it very clear. "You're a bit handy with that cattle prod."

"Come on, you two." Bernie was acting as peacemaker now. "It's only a few hours to wait, and then we can collect our bonuses. All we need is patience."

Don agreed and climbed into the van for what promised to be a very uncomfortable few hours. He had earlier purchased beers for the journey, which was at least some good news! Alcoholic beverages would help to make the time spent sandwiched together slightly more palatable. Bernie dozed off quite quickly but, after drinking more alcohol than was wise, Dave started a conversation that chilled Don to the bone.

"I'm sorry, Don. I've been a pain in the neck on this trip and haven't treated you right. You're a decent sort and know your stuff, but there's things you need to be aware of." Dave was speaking quietly and appeared to be really contrite as he continued. "On the hillside, I had those dogs beat, trust me. After whacking two of the brutes, the only one left capable of causing trouble was the Great Dane, and I figured I could take him as well. But then — this other dog appeared.

"It was the nastiest looking animal I've ever seen, I can tell you. It looked more like an angry bear than a dog. It teamed up with the Great Dane, saw off those useless Dobermans, and then walked towards me. I ain't no coward, Don. I raised my club, but this animal kept on coming. It should've been terrified, but it wasn't. This devil just wouldn't stop. I've been in enough scraps in my life to read an opponent's eyes, and I'm telling you, this dog had smelled fear and was going to kill me, I swear. I backed off and ran. Thank god it didn't come after me. I'm just telling you, mate. If you see this dog, get the hell away from it. It's a killer."

After a few more beers, Dave dropped into an alcohol-fuelled stupor, leaving Don awake and feeling apprehensive. He looked over at the two men, slumped together on the front seat and then swigged from the bottle again.

Then he breathed the words, "Don't teach me how to suck eggs, Dave. I already know how to run."

Chapter Twenty-Three

The Conversation

Whilst the drama of Trevor's capture and incarceration was being played out on a deserted beach, miles from their forest home, Brutus and the Doberman brothers were having their own problems.

Following the mass breakout from the compound just one day ago, the three largest dogs had been tasked with confounding the pursuit by leading the hunters on a wild goose chase through the forest. The Great Dane believed that the group were being tracked by only two young men, neither of whom were particularly suited to the task. If Brutus and his two companions could successfully evade capture, it would buy time for all the other dogs already on the run.

Trevor had asked Brutus to delay their trackers by only a few hours, but, so far, they had managed a whole day. Luther had suggested that they take the fight to the humans, but Brutus, very loyal to Trevor, insisted on following his orders.

After his kidnap, the young and inexperienced Great Dane had acted like a hothead, eager to have a scrap at any price. After escaping from the compound with Trevor and the others, however, he realised the need for a calm disposition. He was thinking more and learning fast. He understood that, should any harm befall either of the men on their trail, it was likely that many more would come after them. On the other hand, if they were able to remain one step ahead of the pursuit, the humans might just admit defeat.

Brutus had no idea what was happening elsewhere but, aided by his new friends, he was determined to stick faithfully to the task entrusted to him.

By late afternoon, a sense of imminent peril had almost overwhelmed him, and so he spoke about it to the others. Both Dobermans dismissed his fears, thinking them irrational. Nonetheless, in an effort to reassure the distressed Great Dane, Lester gave him much of the credit for his successful prosecution of Trevor's plan. After all, they had evaded those tracking them for almost the entire day and had begun to feel confident that these men were unlikely to pose a serious threat in the future. Brutus might have been reassured by Lester's calm insistence about their success, but his worries were not about the criminals. His senses told him that he was being closely watched and by something that was definitely not human.

The big dog needed thinking time, so he sauntered off to contemplate things on his own. He was a powerful animal, even for a Great Dane and, while Poppy did not consider him the smartest dog in the world, he was adapting to his new life and had managed to keep his little pack ahead of their pursuers. In addition, he was strong, fearless and loyal, which, in his own opinion, counted for a lot. He had given Poppy a hard time over the last few days, particularly when they discussed the cat. In all fairness, Brutus had to admit that the Lhasa apso had been right about that subject. He was sure that, of all his new friends, Poppy would have been the one to reassure him if only she had been here. He felt alone, overwhelmed by a growing sense of menace, a foreboding that lingered stubbornly in the back of his mind. Reluctantly and forlornly, he trudged back to join the Doberman brothers waiting for him in the undergrowth.

Meanwhile, not two hundred yards from where Brutus had been standing, almost invisible in the undergrowth, a large dog was watching and waiting. Dima remembered this place from years before when, as a puppy, he had fled from captivity with his one and only friend, the same friend that had betrayed him and left him alone to be recaptured by the very humans who had imprisoned him in the first place.

The Ovcharka heard a low, growling noise and realised the sound was coming from deep within his own throat, something that always happened when his mind drifted back to his troubled past.

A sharp, cracking sound from within the trees above his hiding place startled him, and he looked up into the night sky. Dima was shaken. It hadn't once occurred to him that, while he was watching Brutus, another far more intelligent animal was stalking him. He was angry and ashamed that he had not sensed this unwanted intrusion and raged at the figure high above him, sitting quietly amongst the branches of a huge oak tree. Dima saw that it was a cat, a contemptible, devious and insidious creature. Dogs do not appreciate any animal sneaking up on them in the dark — but a cat? No, No, No.

"What do you want here?" Charmaine was the first to speak.

The dog roared again but did not respond to her question, preferring naked aggression in place of conversation. Charmaine felt relieved to be out of harm's way.

"Why are you watching Brutus?" A tetchy Charmaine spoke again but louder this time.

"Why should I talk to you?" The Ovcharka's voice was deep and controlled. "I've never trusted felines, and even you are no exception."

"*Even* me?" Charmaine replied, emphasising the first word.

"Even you," Dima retorted contemptuously. "The cat who runs with dogs."

"Are you searching for Milo?" Charmaine continued, "because he is not here and won't be back for a long time — maybe never."

The dog reacted angrily to Charmaine's question and snarled loudly. "How do you know what I want? How do you know who I am?" With all control gone, he was shaking with rage now and would have torn her to pieces had she not been well out of reach.

"I know who you are, Ovcharka. I know you are Dima, the dog who craves revenge. Yesterday, you saved Brutus and the others from the humans, and they all love you for it. Brutus believes that you're a hero, but I know better. You're an extraordinarily dangerous animal with a heart of stone, determined to have a reckoning." Charmaine was angry now.

Dima's mood darkened, and he looked up at this disrespectful creature and spoke to her with words as cold as ice. "I didn't know Milo was with your friends when I helped them, but I know it now. You will not see me again, feline. I need no help to find Milo... or should I say, Trevor?"

Charmaine was not easily rattled by anything but was struggling for a reply. She could not believe that this cold-hearted and merciless beast could have had any friends, let alone a dog like Trevor. The cat wanted to know more about the Ovcharka's intentions, but the opportunity was lost because Dima stared into her eyes for a few seconds and then turned and crashed back through the undergrowth until he was out of sight.

Following this angry confrontation, Charmaine remained where she was, hoping that Trevor was safe and that Dima would not be able to find him.

A short distance away, Brutus, completely unaware of what had just taken place, suddenly relaxed. For the time being, at least, the feelings of a malevolent presence close at hand were gone.

Chapter Twenty-Four

Dima

Seething with rage, the massive Ovcharka growled angrily as he put some distance between himself and the meddlesome feline. He strode purposefully through the dense undergrowth, thinking only of confronting his erstwhile friend Milo, the Patterdale terrier, now known by an entirely different name.

Despite a pronounced limp, the lasting legacy of injuries he had suffered as a puppy, Dima made excellent progress over the challenging terrain even though walking long distances had become more painful of late. In spite of these difficulties, the huge dog was driven to find his former friend and would go to extraordinary lengths to catch up with him. Dima's size and ursine features terrified people, obliging him to travel during the hours of darkness. In this way, he avoided, as far as possible, any contact with humans. He had become a nocturnal predator and was a proud and fearless beast, unafraid of almost any other animal, regardless of size or strength. He was wary of humans; however, over the years, he had studied their methods and learnt the many ways in which they had tried to track him. This precious knowledge had enabled him to remain one step ahead of anyone who would try to enslave him.

As Dima followed the winding path through the bowels of the forest, he recalled the significant events of his troubled past. The Ovcharka had been born into a cruel world where pain and suffering proved to be an everyday occurrence. His so-called masters knew the power of his breed and foolishly considered that, when fully grown and trained, he would make a very effective guard dog. This was a decision they would later regret.

Given his history, it was not difficult to understand his excessive hostility and vindictiveness, not only towards Milo but to any human or animal that crossed his path. He remembered, with extraordinary clarity, his first escape from captivity on the night of the great storm. On that occasion, Milo, whom he had trusted with his life, had helped him to escape, only to desert him later and leave him at the mercy of malicious humans who enthusiastically exacted their revenge. In the Ovcharka's opinion, his friend's freedom had been gained at Dima's expense, and now Milo had to pay the price.

Dima's freedom had taken another two years to secure, from which time he had plotted his revenge on the men who had treated him so cruelly. He had now become a solitary fugitive, relentlessly pursued whenever he was seen, but always learning and perfecting the skills required for eluding those who would hound him. The feisty cat had caused Dima to lose his temper and even question his own sanity. He could not understand why a feline should be concerned about the fate of a dog, especially a worthless Patterdale like Milo. He stopped to think for a moment. If this cat was willing to protect Milo, how many others might line up in his defence?

His thoughts drifted back a couple of days to a heated confrontation on the hill between a pack of unknown dogs and two vicious humans. Perhaps unwisely, he had intervened in this violent encounter, recalling specifically the sense of camaraderie between all the pack members. On that day, he had saved these dogs by fighting alongside a huge Great Dane after one of the men had badly injured two of the canine combatants. Not wishing to be delayed, the Ovcharka had left the area immediately afterwards.

A dog like Dima travelled alone, content to survive by his own wits. He had no idea why he had become involved in this particular fight, but the truth was that, beneath his aggressive and volatile nature, he had a good heart and abhorred injustice. Moreover, he despised humans with a passion, even more than he hated his arch-nemesis. Thanks to the cat, the Ovcharka now realised that Milo had been there that day and that he had inadvertently saved his life. He heard that growl once more and felt his anger rise again.

Milo had always been the smart one, particularly when they were both puppies. He was forever testing the boundaries of human patience and causing their masters as many problems as he could. He was just a small puppy and, to protect him, Dima would step in and not only take the blame for these misdemeanours but the punishment as well.

After Dima's escape and subsequent recapture, life for the Ovcharka puppy became unbearable. The men in charge beat him regularly and, on occasion, deprived him of food and water for days. For two years, he paid the price, not only for his own escape but for Milo's escape too. They tried everything to break him but failed due to his indomitable spirit. As Dima grew in size and strength, he watched and waited for the opportunity to escape and, when it came, he took it and broke free. He had become an unstoppable force, especially in regard to his dogged pursuit of Milo.

In the beginning, alone in the wild, he struggled to survive but used every setback and disappointment to educate himself. He learned that if he stayed away from men, they would not bother him, particularly if he moved from one area to another under cover of darkness. On the rare occasions that Dima travelled during the day, it was a different story, simply because a huge feral dog crossing the country alone and unsupervised always attracted the wrong kind of attention. He would normally lie low until it was dark and then move on. To any humans attempting to track him at night, the Ovcharka's ability to blend into the shadows made the prospect of confronting him both terrifying and extremely dangerous.

A sudden breeze startled Dima, and he realised he had reached the outer limits of the forest. He was unfamiliar with the terrain here but, after sniffing the earth all around the path, he picked up a scent that indicated that a number of dogs had passed this point not too long ago. His mood lightened, and he sat, considering his next step. He realised that he had no alternative other than to follow the scent because it would diminish over time, thus denying him the opportunity to find these dogs. Even if Milo wasn't with them, one of the group might know his whereabouts. Dima was only too painfully aware that he might be chasing shadows but, after a few more minutes of reflection, he stood up, sniffed the air and then followed the trail across the fields. There was no other viable alternative.

By the time the Ovcharka reached the outskirts of the town, it was becoming light. Accordingly, he chose to bide his time and seek a secluded spot where he could recuperate safely until nightfall. He noted a small area of trees and bushes away from the path, ideal for this purpose. The scent of dogs was strong in this area, and he quickly realised that his quarry had also stopped here. This was exceptionally frustrating for Dima, but the respite was necessary if he was to successfully follow this trail and locate the Patterdale. What did twelve hours matter when he was so close to a final resolution? There would now be a chance to encounter his former friend and have the reckoning that had dominated his thoughts for so many years.

Chapter Twenty-Five

Poppy's Plan

"Wake up, little dog. It's time." Oscar was gently tapping the top of Poppy's head. We have to go, right now."

Poppy looked up at the stern-looking face staring down at her and felt momentarily disoriented. "What about making a plan?" she asked, still gathering her thoughts.

"You don't have to worry about that," growled Oscar. "It's all sorted. We'll fill you in on the way."

Poppy wasn't impressed but remained silent on the subject, hoping that Oscar and his friends had truly understood the difficulties involved in releasing her friends from a locked van. They had all assured her that they had done this sort of thing before, and successfully too, but admitted to her that it had always been under the instruction and supervision of their human masters.

As they travelled across the fields, Oscar, the smartest of her three allies, ran through the supposedly foolproof way in which they would effect a rescue. In Poppy's opinion, it was not really a plan at all, and their efforts were clearly destined to fail. As Oscar continued his monotone delivery, she became even more depressed by what appeared to be the complete and utter hopelessness of the chosen strategy.

She waited patiently until Oscar had finished and then spoke to all three, quietly but very clearly. "So, boys! The basis of your master plan is to wait until the humans get out of the van and then attack them as they open the back doors. This, you believe, will enable Trevor and the others to jump out and escape. You will then lead us all away from the beach and hide us in a secure location nearby. Incidentally, a location that you haven't yet found. Are you all out of your mind? This plan, for what it's worth, will fail because it relies on these humans doing exactly what you need them to do, and that is very unlikely to happen. In the first place, the men might not even open the back door of the van but just drive away instead. What do you intend to do then, Oscar? Wave them goodbye after wishing them bon voyage!"

Poppy's brutal assessment thoroughly dismayed the trio, but she felt it was deserved. Oscar was not happy with her language and showed it by growling loudly and unpleasantly in her face.

"Complain all you like, Oscar. I'm not frightened of you, and I intend to have my say," Poppy continued defiantly. "Tell me. Have any of you ever done something like this before tonight? Well, have you? Because I have, and I believe that we are going to need a little more than

211

brute force and good luck to succeed. At least consider my opinion. For example, what if they attack us first? What if they have weapons? Humans have things that can hurt us really badly, and we'll only have one chance. Please, please listen to me because, out there, you will not have any good humans to protect you. Understand one thing, it is solely down to the four of us to rescue my friends, and I won't countenance failure."

Oscar and the other two dogs looked stunned. Confident as they were, they hadn't even considered that she might have a better plan. Poppy could see by their faces that they were beginning to take her seriously.

"All right, Poppy," said Victor. "What do you suggest? But be quick because the water is leaving the beach right now, and the humans will be in a position to depart very soon."

At last, these stubborn males were finally getting it. Poppy thought about it for a minute and considered what Trevor would do in these circumstances. The ability to make a coherent and successful plan on the move was difficult, but an idea was already forming in the little dog's head. She quickly ran through the details with the others, and they seemed to like it. Even Oscar agreed to let her take charge.

In a little more than five minutes, the four dogs were running down the stone steps leading to the beach. The water had indeed receded, leaving the van a clear route back over the sand to the road. There was as yet no sign of movement in the van, thus giving them time to prepare for action. Oscar moved to a concealed position only yards from the rear doors. Romeo and Victor were tasked with finding a hiding place amongst the dark seaweed which lay abundantly all around the rocky enclave. Poppy remained exactly where she was, approximately twenty feet in front of the van. All the dogs settled down to wait. Poppy could see that all three men were slumped in the front seats. Oscar and the others were ready. She was ready. It was time.

After only a few moments, Poppy heard voices that became progressively louder as the three men stumbled out of the van. As soon as Bernie clapped eyes on Poppy, she was ready. She howled loudly, making sure he had recognised her before she ran straight to the rocks where Trevor and the others had earlier concealed themselves.

After the initial shock of seeing the Lhasa apso, Dave and Don gave chase, leaving only Bernie with the van. Poppy raced into the rocks, desperately hoping that her pursuers would follow. She even slowed down a little, allowing the two men to gain some ground on her. Just as they were almost upon her, Poppy veered away sharply to the right and darted into the rocky enclave closely followed by both men — just as she had hoped.

213

Behind her, she could hear their laboured breathing brought on by this sudden exertion and even had time to turn and look at her pursuers before heading for the little gap. It seemed tighter this time, and the little dog felt panic overtake her when she almost became stuck. Eventually, she squeezed through the narrow space and made good her escape. She then headed straight back to the van at speed.

The humans were now searching the rocks but obviously couldn't find her. They gave up quite quickly and returned to the entrance, where they were confronted by two angry German shepherds, snapping and snarling at them. At first, the humans didn't know what to do. They stepped back and remained trapped within the rocks. Of course, this was all according to plan, leaving Bernie, the only remaining obstacle, standing at the rear of the van, waiting for his cronies to return.

He looked quite shocked when Poppy appeared in front of him, but he stayed calm. He wasn't worried about a little dog like her.

"Hello, Poppy. Fancy you being here," he crowed. "This is a bonus for us. Why don't you join your friends inside?"

Bernie turned the door handle and opened the back door, but only by an inch or two. She watched as he reached into his coat and pulled out a cattle prod.

"Come on, girl. Just a little closer." He was waiting patiently, his hand gripping the weapon which he moved from side to side. He turned his head back and shouted to his companions.

"The Lhasa's here, guys. Must have been here all the time. I've got her now."

He sounded very pleased with himself and moved slowly and deliberately towards the little dog, the weapon still held firmly in his right hand. Poppy growled at him, but Bernie just laughed whilst clumsily lunging forward and falling headlong into the sand. He tried to stand up but was prevented from doing so by a second, larger dog growling at him. Bernie was not the heroic type but foolishly decided to stand up and fight. As he regained his feet and raised his weapon to strike, Oscar closed his jaws on Bernie's arm and took him back down.

Once satisfied that Bernie no longer presented a threat, Poppy called out to Trevor, who pushed the van door open and jumped down beside her. Charlie and Flora followed.

"Great work, Poppy," Trevor said." Now we have to get out of here."

Oscar released Bernie's arm and stepped away from him.

"Follow me," he said to Trevor. And, in no time at all, they were climbing up the stone steps and running across the fields. Bernie had wisely decided not to give chase.

As soon as the party was able to stop, Poppy snapped at Oscar. "What about Romeo and Victor? Did you see what happened?"

"They'll be fine," Oscar said gruffly. "They both know how to look after themselves."

It seems they did because both returned to the main group shortly thereafter for the brief journey home.

All the way back, Oscar and Trevor were deep in conversation. Whilst Poppy could not make out what they were saying, she knew instinctively that Trevor would be doing most of the talking.

Later on, the Patterdale spoke quietly to Poppy, apologising for getting his strategy so wrong. "What can I say to you, Poppy?" he said. "Maybe I am losing my touch."

Poppy didn't really have a chance to reply because they had arrived at Oscar's little shed as dawn was breaking. There was plenty of food and drink to be had, and they all made the most of it. Poppy felt relieved that her plan had worked, but she had learned not to be complacent. This appeared to be just as well because, as the dogs were starting to relax, a large shadow fell across the floor. A human shadow.

Chapter Twenty-Six

The Policeman and the Vet

Former police constable Geoff Brown appeared in the doorway, troubled by the sight of four unfamiliar dogs standing anxiously in his shed.

"Well, what have we got here then, boys?"

On this particular morning, he had been woken by loud and continuous barking coming from the shed and had rushed out to investigate. Upon his arrival, the barking stopped, and seven dogs, four of them unknown to him, immediately turned their heads in his direction. Geoff was surprised and not a little unnerved by this totally unexpected turn of events, even though the four strangers remained motionless in front of him. His own dogs, three German shepherds, stood in silence as he asked his rhetorical question.

Geoff was a thoughtful and intelligent man, but it took the ex-police officer quite a few minutes to process the unusual spectacle right in front of his eyes. He had spent twenty-five years of his life in the Metropolitan Police and had only recently retired. After years involved in the seedier side of big city police work, Geoff had felt the need for a little solitude and quiet reflection. With this in mind, he had taken the decision to relocate from London to a small cottage on the Devon coast.

During his final years of service, he had worked as a dog handler, a job he had absolutely adored. In light of his affinity for dogs, he had been offered one of three recently-retired German shepherds. Not wishing to separate them, he decided to take all three, something he had never regretted.

The tension was broken by one of the dogs, a self-assured Patterdale terrier, which stepped forward confidently and stood facing him. None of the remaining canines moved a muscle. The silence was palpable and, for a few difficult moments, Geoff just stood there staring blankly at the Patterdale whilst intermittently looking at his own dogs for support — but receiving none. There was no aggression, only a hushed and restrained standoff.

After a few minutes of this stalemate, Geoff just shrugged his shoulders, left the shed and closed and locked the door after him.

Inside the shed, Trevor became angry and turned on Oscar. "What's going on, Oscar? I understood that you're allowed to come and go as you please, but here you are locked up with us. I trusted you, but you've let us all down."

Oscar protested. "No Trevor, no! The door has always been left open for us. I've told you the truth. All three of us are really well looked after and have always had the freedom to do whatever we want. We have never been confined or mistreated."

Romeo and Victor both felt the same way and persuaded Trevor to remain calm and wait upon events. As the shed door had been locked, Trevor had no alternative but to wait for Geoff's return even though he didn't like it. Feral dogs face hardship and strife every day of their lives but thrive on being free to roam wherever and whenever they choose. Consequently, the resourceful Patterdale, and his friend Charlie, remained anxious and felt vulnerable due to their inability to escape this confinement. Aware of Trevor's discomfiture, Poppy moved closer to him, doing her best to calm him while assuring him that they would soon be free to move.

Fortunately, about an hour later, Geoff returned to the shed, once again closing the door behind him. He looked at each dog in turn and then examined a sheet of paper in his hand. Whilst the dogs had been locked in the shed, Geoff had contacted the local police station about the new arrivals and was surprised to learn that officers were already aware that four stray dogs were on the loose. Apparently, a local man had been walking his dogs on the beach earlier in the day when something had spooked them, and all four had fled. More importantly, according to the man, he considered that his dogs might represent a threat to the public.

Geoff read from the paper again and shrugged his shoulders.

"A French bulldog, a Chihuahua, a Lhasa apso and a Patterdale. That's very strange. Four dangerous dogs hiding in my shed. Well! None of you look very threatening to me."

Nonetheless, he picked up a length of rope from a hook on the shed wall and moved towards Trevor. "Sorry boy, but I have to secure all the dogs, starting with you. It's pretty obvious to me that you're in charge and, where you go, the others will follow."

Poppy immediately stepped in front of Trevor and growled fiercely. Geoff was not greatly impressed.

"It's no good, little one. I really am sorry, but I have been asked to keep you all here until someone shows up to collect you."

Again the human moved towards Trevor, who began to back away, eventually finding himself trapped in a corner. What happened next surprised them all, including Geoff, because Oscar strode over and stood in front of his master, angrily growling at him. Geoff was confused now and quietly tried to calm his dog and encourage him to move out of the way. Unfortunately for Geoff, this ploy was ineffective, and Oscar maintained his defiant stance.

At this point, the human began to speak in a far more aggressive tone that merely prompted both Victor and Romeo to move into positions on either side of Oscar. Geoff's dogs now presented a formidable triple threat which was certainly too much for one man.

Poppy was really worried now because the situation had begun to spiral out of control. She needn't have worried, however, because Geoff just sat back on the floor and shook his head. He didn't seem to be angry anymore. He looked at Trevor again and smiled.

"Who are you that my dogs want to protect you? Even though I am sure they don't know you. You're most certainly a very intriguing animal."

Poppy recognised that Trevor had not been around humans for a long time and might lack her insight. It seemed to behove her to take charge. This human was not a bad man, but he didn't know their history. She reasoned that if Oscar helped catch bad humans, then this particular human should be someone she could trust. Poppy trotted over and licked his hand. She could tell that he was surprised, and he patted her gently on the head.

"All right, girl, all right. Don't worry. We have a bit of a situation here, don't we? My dogs are telling me something about you and your friends, but I can't understand what it is. What should I do?"

Poppy had his attention now and turned toward Oscar.

"Oscar. Please do exactly as I say. All three of you must move away now." Poppy emphasised the last word.

To Geoff's complete surprise, Oscar stood up and walked back to his normal place in the shed, closely followed by the other two.

Absolute shock replaced surprise as Geoff, stunned by what was happening, found himself barely able to speak. "Who are you, really? I mean, what do you want me to do? You seem to have control of my own dogs now, and I'm powerless to do anything about it."

Trevor quietly thanked Poppy for her help and turned his head towards the shed door.

Geoff saw him do it. "You want me to let you go?" he said abruptly. "I just open the door and let you go. Is that it?"

Trevor turned back to the door again and then looked at Geoff. Poppy knew what that look was like. No dog or human was immune to Trevor's stare.

The man rose, walked over to the door and opened it. Poppy jumped up, ready to leave, but Trevor firmly told her to stay put and keep quiet. She did as she was told. She rarely argued with Trevor.

The man was still standing by the open door with a quizzical expression on his face. "You clearly want to leave, but you are not leaving. You're now acting as if you want to stay." He was puzzled at first, but then the penny finally dropped, and he laughed. "I think I understand you now, Mr Patterdale. You want to stay here until you decide to leave, which means you're telling me that this door must be left open."

As the man finished speaking, Trevor whimpered, then just sank to the floor and remained motionless. Poppy was panic-stricken and looked at the man, imploring him to do something. Trevor was hurt, and something had to be done. Geoff moved very quickly and examined Trevor, who appeared to be out cold on the floor. Poppy would have liked to have told the man about the injuries Trevor had sustained since leaving the forest but could only whimper loudly instead. All the other dogs were unsettled too. The human raced out of the shed and into the house.

After a very short time, he returned carrying a cloth and some water and tended to the unconscious dog stretched out on the floor. Shortly thereafter, a young woman arrived carrying a bag which she placed beside Trevor. She then examined him using items that she removed from her bag.

"He has a serious burn on his side, Geoff," the new arrival said. "It looks electrical, but that doesn't seem to be the only injury. I think this dog might have received a blow to the head and will need a lot of care in the next few days. I just don't understand how he's managed to keep going for so long."

"Would it be possible to check the dog's chip, Hannah? I have questions about these dogs, and it would help me if I could establish ownership. I don't know why, but I feel really uneasy about all this."

"Well. You can forget this one," Hannah said, glancing at Trevor. "Look at him. No one owns this dog." She raised her arm and pointed to the shed door. "He lives out there, that's for sure, possibly with other dogs, including the Chihuahua here. They're both more or less wild, if I'm not mistaken. I know the look, Geoff. I've seen enough feral dogs in my time to be confident that I'm correct, but I'll check them anyway. As for the other two, both are domesticated and have been well cared for."

Geoff took in what he was being told and turned back to Trevor.

"Will you allow me to look after you for a few days then, boy? With that injury, you won't be going far."

Trevor didn't respond to what was being said and just lay there, clearly distressed and in pain. As the young vet finished her brief examination of all four dogs, she wrote two numbers on a notepad that she took from her bag.

"I was right, Geoff. Two with chips and two without. I'll come back to you about this."

Geoff asked her what needed to be done and then promised to look after all of the dogs until the Patterdale was fit again. Even Poppy seemed able to understand what was happening and sat beside Trevor as he drifted into unconsciousness. Geoff did what he could to make

Trevor comfortable and then left him in the care of his friends.

After all the comings and goings during the last few hours, the dogs were exhausted but took it in turns, nonetheless, to watch over their injured leader.

It was in the early hours of the morning that Poppy finally succumbed to her exhaustion and fell into a deep sleep.

Chapter Twenty-Seven

Fight or Flight

In the period following Poppy's kidnap, the young Lhasa apso had lost all sense of safety and security. During this time, she had found life extraordinarily difficult but, with Trevor's help, she had come through it and survived. Now, within the secure walls of the little shed that Geoff had created for his own dogs, and surrounded by friends, she could finally relax without the threat of violence or mayhem.

All the dogs, exhausted by their recent tribulations, were content to be in a safe place under the protection of a man that she believed to be a good human. For Poppy, there was now less to worry about and much to look forward to. She cast a glance towards Trevor, who was sleeping soundly and remained unaware of her feelings. As she drifted off to sleep, her thoughts, as usual, returned to home and the love, warmth and comfort that were dear to her.

Poppy awoke early the following morning and realised that both Trevor and Charlie were absent. In a state of high anxiety, she raised the alarm, demanding an immediate search for the missing dogs. Flora stood up, visibly shaken by the news, cowering by her bed and mumbling incoherently. Oscar and his two friends were struggling to gather their wits when Poppy lost patience with them and stormed out of the shed on her own. She was certain that Trevor and Charlie would never desert their friends and so became extremely concerned for their wellbeing.

Once outside in the garden, she heard a familiar voice.

It was Charlie, standing alone by the stone wall. "Hold on a minute, Poppy. I'll come with you. Let's have a look around on our own. It'll be fun."

"Fun, do you think, Charlie?" she replied caustically. "Trevor is missing, and all you can think about is your own amusement!"

"He's fine, Poppy," Charlie replied dismissively. "The big man looked in on Trevor early this morning but couldn't settle him. Eventually, he took him up to the house, and they both went inside. Trevor's in a nice place and is being looked after."

"And how do you know this?" Poppy asked Charlie indignantly.

"Because I followed them, of course. You know, Poppy, you're not the only dog around here who cares! I've been with Trevor from the very beginning, and I can't tell you how much he means to me. Before I met him, I had been beaten by humans so badly that I could hardly stand and then abandoned to starve. Trevor found me dying in the forest, tended to me, fed me and stayed with me until I recovered. He saved my life, Poppy. In those days, there were only two of us, and we made a great team. Trevor is being cared for, I promise. And remember, this stranger could've locked us in the shed, but he didn't, did he? I'm sure he is one of the good people, Poppy."

Reluctantly, she agreed but needed to make sure Trevor really was all right. So, they both trotted up to the house and stood by the huge glass door. Trevor was still in bed and looked comfortable. There was a large bowl of water and some food next to his bed. Poppy tried tapping at the door with her paw, but Trevor didn't hear. Charlie barked at the door, but he didn't hear that either.

Just as they were about to give up, Geoff came up behind them and pulled the door open. "Go on in, you two. See if you can cheer your friend up. He's still a little groggy."

Poppy didn't need to understand Geoff. She jumped through the open door and ran to Trevor, closely followed by Charlie. Trevor opened his eyes.

"Are you all right, Trevor?" she gasped, talking very quickly. "What can I do? Tell me the plan."

"Slow down, Poppy," Trevor responded calmly. "I am not fit to go anywhere at present, but I'm being looked after and should be well enough to leave in a day or two.

For now, keep alert and be ready to run if you have to. This man is a friend, I'm sure, but take nothing for granted."

With that, Trevor closed his eyes again and was asleep in seconds.

The two dogs wanted to remain, but Geoff made it clear that they should leave Trevor alone and allow him to recuperate. Both dogs understood that he would only be able to return to the shed when fully fit. They had no choice but to respond to Geoff's wishes and leave Trevor in peace.

Oscar was talking when they got back to the shed and immediately turned his attention to Poppy. "What's happening, Poppy?" Oscar asked. "Please assure us that Trevor is alright."

Happily, she was able to confirm that Trevor, although still quite weak, was indeed in good spirits and would be back with them shortly. Meanwhile, they must remain alert because the criminals were still at large.

During the time spent in the company of Geoff's dogs, the fugitives had the freedom to go wherever they wanted, with no exception. Oscar, or one of the other members of Geoff's trio, always accompanied the smaller dogs when they needed to explore the garden or have a run on the beach. This was just in case the criminals were still around, albeit none of them had been seen for a while. Quite naturally, given their feelings of wellbeing and security, they began to unwind and even enjoy themselves a little.

Every now and then, Poppy and Charlie would trot up to the house to see Trevor and check on his progress. Sometimes, when the weather was very warm, Geoff would leave the big glass door open, and they would just walk right in. Trevor was always glad to see them and hear the latest news.

On the fourth day, a shabby white van pulled onto the drive in front of Geoff's house, and two very familiar men emerged and went inside. This was the very van that Poppy had been thrown into after being snatched from her home, and here it was again. The same two men were back, swaggering up Geoff's drive, apparently more than willing to take all the dogs back into captivity.

Poppy was terrified and raced to the shed to alert the others, but Charlie and Flora had also been watching and already knew what was happening. There seemed to be no alternative but to run, even if it meant leaving Trevor behind. It seemed pretty obvious to Poppy that Geoff had betrayed them all, but despite her suspicions, she tried to remain calm.

"The hunters are in the house," she said, "and we don't have a lot of time. If we escape to the beach, Charlie, we can hide out until dark and then move on from there."

"What about Trevor?" Charlie muttered. "I won't leave without him, Poppy, and you won't persuade me to do otherwise."

"Maybe you won't have to do anything." Oscar interrupted their conversation. "Look out there."

While the three friends had been talking, a second vehicle arrived on the drive and stopped immediately behind the first. This was an unexpected development because they had no idea what was going on and were understandably alarmed. As they looked on, two men they hadn't seen before stepped out of the second vehicle and approached the front door. They glanced briefly towards the shed and then entered the building as soon as the door was opened.

Distressed by these new arrivals, Poppy and her two friends expected to be handed over to the criminals at any time.

Poppy looked at Charlie. "We've got to get away from here, Charlie.

Charlie looked back at her. "Not this time, Poppy. I'm tired of running, and anyway, I'm not leaving Trevor here on his own."

"It may not come to that," interrupted Oscar, standing between Romeo and Victor. "We all trust Geoff, and so must you. We will not let you leave and create more danger for yourselves. It's for your own good."

With those words, the three larger dogs blocked the shed door. Poppy could do nothing.

"I trust Geoff too, you know, Poppy," Charlie spoke quietly but in a reassuring tone. "Oscar is right. If we leave now, we won't have a chance. Without Trevor, we'll be caught anyway, so what's the point of running?"

Poppy didn't have a chance to respond to Charlie. She could hear raised voices and turned towards the sound. Victor and the others moved away from the door, allowing Poppy to see what was going on. She was shocked to see all the men emerge from the house and walk to the second van. Poppy noticed that both Dave and Bernie looked very worried and had their hands fastened behind their backs.

"What's happening, Oscar?" Poppy asked nervously.

"When I caught bad humans," Oscar declared, "they usually ended up like that."

This was very exciting, and Poppy couldn't wait to tell Trevor the news, but she had a niggling feeling that her nightmare was far from over. Importantly, where was the third member of the gang who had chased them on the beach last week — the man who had hurt Trevor with that metal stick?

Poppy had no chance to dwell on the whereabouts of the third man because Trevor was hobbling towards her, still looking a little frail but nonetheless much better than when she had last seen him.

"Let's go back to the shed," he said softly. "I can tell you everything there."

Once all the dogs had settled down again, Trevor explained that the two humans from the compound had come to the house intent, he believed, on taking all four dogs back into captivity.

"At first, the men were just talking, but then two more humans came in, Geoff's friends, I think, and there was a lot of shouting. Then the newcomers overpowered the villains and pinned their hands behind their backs. After it was all over, I realised that Geoff must know our story because I fervently believe that we are all safe now."

Poppy desperately wanted to trust Trevor but remained uneasy about the third man who had not been seen since that awful night on the beach.

Later, after they had all eaten, Geoff came down to the shed and took Trevor back to the house. In fact, unbeknown to Poppy, he was taking him to see his friend Hannah, the vet who had examined Trevor a few days earlier.

For Poppy, it had been a very exciting day, and she felt a mixture of exhilaration and exhaustion. She was acutely aware, however, that her earlier actions had upset their three bodyguards, and some humble pie had to be eaten.

"I'm really very sorry, Oscar," Poppy spoke quietly and from the heart. "You were right, and I was wrong. Geoff has been kind to all of us since we arrived, and I should have trusted him, but I was afraid, and this affected my judgement."

On behalf of all three, Oscar grudgingly accepted her apology but remained in a grouchy mood.

Later, the three German shepherds decided to take a run along the beach, although Poppy, Charlie and Flora were not asked to accompany them. After they had gone, Poppy settled down with the others for a well-deserved rest. Unfortunately, it didn't last long because she was disturbed by an unfamiliar noise on the other side of the shed door. Poppy sniffed the air and sensed danger.

Chapter Twenty-Eight

The Dog-Catcher Returns

Don Davis, the devious dog warden, loitered menacingly in the doorway of Geoff Brown's garden shed, a quick-release grasper in his right hand. Impatient to do what needed to be done, he remained fully aware of the precarious nature of his situation.

Earlier in the day, his two cronies, Dave Dixon and Bernie French, had been questioned by police on suspicion of dog theft but released without charge after only a couple of hours in custody. Both men had told the same barely credible story about protecting local people from dangerous feral dogs running amok in the countryside. In the absence of any real evidence to the contrary, it was not deemed to be a crime, so no further action was recommended. After all, it was a busy police station, and officers had recently been dealing with a spate of burglaries.

After being released, Dave refused to take any further part in the recapture of the dogs, not least because the police now had his name and crime sheet, putting him at risk of a speedy return to prison if he was caught again. On the other hand, Bernie was happy to see the job through and teamed up with Don in an effort to catch these wretched dogs and return them to the Greys. His decision was based on the expectation of a successful outcome when he would be rewarded by his employers and, perhaps finally, be given the respect he deserved.

Later that afternoon, Bernie, accompanied by the dog warden, drove back to Geoff's isolated property to assess their chances of stealing back the four fugitive dogs. After watching Geoff's house for a while, their patience finally paid dividends. Don sniggered to himself as Brown emerged from the house, placed the Patterdale on the back seat of his car and drove off. This left only three remaining obstacles, the German shepherds — feisty dogs that had given Don much cause for concern.

Fortunately, his anxieties were partially allayed when all three suddenly burst out of the garden and bounded across the grass towards the beach. The two men realised they had to be quick and so waited for only a few minutes before Bernie carefully reversed the van onto the drive as close to the house as possible. Whilst doing so, they laughed aloud as it dawned on them that this might well be their lucky day. Of course, the icing on the cake would have been to collar the Patterdale, but that particular animal was presently out of their reach and likely to remain so. For now, the two men were content to recapture the Lhasa and the French bulldog and return them to the Greys, who they imagined would be extremely grateful. The Chihuahua was an unexpected bonus.

A self-satisfied grin spread across Don's face as he contemplated the reward he might be offered as a result of his loyal service. As far as he was concerned, everything looked set fair for him to come out of this very well. He instructed Bernie to wait in the van while he had a good look around. As the dog handler reached the shed, he readied himself on the other side of the open doorway.

Inside the shed, the anxious occupants crouched quietly, waiting and watching in the gloom. Poppy was on full alert and growling quietly.

Flora spoke softly. "What's the matter, Poppy? You're frightening me now."

"Just be ready to run," Poppy whispered before turning to Charlie, who was already alert.

Charlie had been living on his wits for much longer than Poppy and knew as much as Trevor about the dangers surrounding them. The Lhasa sensed danger but remained determined to go down fighting.

The silhouette of a man appeared in the doorway and, as Poppy watched intently, he stepped inside quietly, closing the door behind him. All three dogs remained motionless as if frozen in time. The human was clutching a long pole with a loose collar at one end, and his breathing was heavy and laboured. Whilst the dog-catcher's eyes adjusted to the sudden change in the light, Poppy was able to get a good look at him. and immediately recognised him as the third member of the gang who had trapped Trevor on the beach only days ago. Furthermore, she was certain she had confronted this human even prior to that. Yes, of course, he was the unpleasant man in the old lady's garden. On that occasion, Trevor and Poppy had escaped after receiving valuable assistance from the lady in question, who had armed herself with a poker. No such help existed here.

The three friends had nowhere to hide and no way to break free. They were trapped, and to make matters worse, none of them were fighting dogs, thus making it an easy snatch for the hunter.

Poppy looked at her adversary again and remembered how Trevor had suffered because of his actions.

Reluctantly, she was about to surrender herself when Charlie called out, "Don't give up, Poppy! When you get the chance, get away from here and don't stop running."

Don looked down at the three dogs standing resolutely before him, watching his every move. He felt the weight of the grasper in his hand and moved forward. Poppy glared at him as he brandished the metal pole while holding the shed door closed with his free hand. Poppy wondered how he could catch and secure three dogs without any help from his violent friends? She moved cautiously towards him, turning from side to side, and keeping her head and body low in an attempt to avoid the collar he was waving in front of her face — but what next? What could she possibly do now that would save them?

Suddenly, there was a heavy crash as something slammed into the back wall of the shed with enough force to cause the whole structure to shake. This terrified the dog-catcher and the three young animals within, although this was only the beginning of their ordeal. The resounding thud immediately claimed the attention of all the occupants of the shed, but it was followed by the guttural snarl of a predatory animal apparently poised to attack. Poppy and her two friends shrunk back, each trying to find a place to conceal themselves. The human looked terrified and turned away from the dogs. Every step he took, he looked around anxiously as his sense of panic increased. He recalled Dave's ominous warning about the gigantic dog he had encountered whilst pursuing the Patterdale.

Dave believed this predator to be part of the Patterdale's pack and had warned Don to be on the lookout. He had also cautioned him to abandon any notion of defending himself if confronted by this monster. Don was caught in a paroxysm of terror and felt himself shaking uncontrollably.

Seconds later, an angry roar preceded an even more violent assault against the shed, leaving Don no alternative but to run. The coward stumbled frantically through the doorway and across the garden to the van. Subsequently, Poppy heard the sound of a vehicle starting up and then driving away. The Lhasa looked towards the rear of the shed and watched in amazement as Charlie emerged from the shadows.

"Don't be ridiculous, Poppy," he chuckled. "It wasn't me. I wish I could sound like that."

Poppy looked around. This animal had frightened the stranger so badly that he had run away. Humans didn't usually do anything like that, even though she had to admit that the sounds had been truly terrifying. For a few moments after the human had fled, Poppy and Flora sat in silence, looking every which way and trembling with fear. Charlie sensed their anguish and trotted over.

"Don't worry, you two. The monster has gone. Whatever it was, it had no interest in us, believe me." Charlie was thinking ahead. "Poppy, I can't understand how that man got into the garden without alerting Geoff. We need to find out what is happening."

She followed him out of the shed and up the path to the house, but there didn't seem to be anyone at home — no Geoff and no Trevor.

"What's going on, Poppy?" Charlie was looking to her for answers, but she was as baffled as her friend and could offer no explanation.

She concealed her true feelings from her friend, however. "Don't worry Charlie. They must have gone out. Let's get Flora and find a safe place to hide. It's no longer safe in the shed."

Just outside the open gate, there was a small clump of trees within which the three dogs settled down to wait.

"I'll keep a lookout, Poppy," Flora said. "It really is about time I did something for you and the others."

Charlie wouldn't hear of it, though and, whilst he was grateful to Flora, he had always been the group's lookout and was unwilling to relinquish that role. According to Charlie, Trevor was unwavering in his reliance on the Chihuahua's exceptional sight and hearing. Poppy didn't argue and was happy to wait with Flora, both of them keeping very quiet.

From their concealed position, they couldn't really see a thing, but about an hour later, they did hear a car pull up on the drive. Moments later, Charlie scurried back to tell them that Geoff had returned home. Best of all, Trevor was with him.

This was great news. They raced back to the shed, where they found Trevor and the three German shepherds sitting on the ground talking to each other.

"Oh, there you are!" Trevor called his friends over. "Come in and sit down. Tell us what has happened to you because I'm pretty sure something has."

Flora explained to Trevor about the man who had been outside the shed and had tried to take them.

"It was very exciting, Trevor, but the human was scared off by the sounds of a horrible beast."

Oscar and his friends laughed at the little dog's story — but not Trevor. He wanted to know much more.

"Did you see anything, Flora?" Trevor was not a dog who frightened easily, but there was something in the way that he stared directly into Flora's eyes that struck terror into Poppy's heart.

"Have you come across this animal in the past, Trevor?" interjected Poppy, "because Oscar can laugh all he likes, but he wasn't there."

Trevor didn't reply, and from the expression on his face, he wasn't going to, something to which she had become very well accustomed. If the Patterdale didn't wish to elaborate, he would close off any further conversation.

Later, when everything had calmed down, Trevor told them where he had been taken and whom he had seen.

"Do you remember the lady who helped me when I was really unwell, Poppy? Well, it seems that I'm almost fully recovered."

Poppy looked at Trevor quizzically and said, "How do you know that?"

Well, alright then, Poppy. I don't understand all human language, of course, but they both seemed to be happy about my condition. They were also talking about you and Flora, I think. Unfortunately, I don't know any more than that, but they seemed to be very pleased with themselves. I trust Geoff, Poppy, and I believe that we will be safe here for the time being. Let's just stay for a few more days, and then, as I promised, I will get you and Flora home."

Chapter Twenty-Nine

The Reckoning

It was a brand new day. Feeling secure, Poppy could hear the sound of high winds and torrential rain outside the shed, but she was not prepared to be cooped up any longer. Stultified by inactivity and the apparent lethargy of her friends, she decided to brave the appalling weather by trotting through the open door into the garden. She selected a spot, partially sheltered from the elements and hunkered down to think. As she did so, the sound of a vehicle coming up the lane disturbed her deliberations. The little dog looked in the direction of the noise and watched as a large blue car approached the house and turned into the open gate onto Geoff's drive.

The vehicle contained two human occupants, a woman at the wheel and a man in the passenger seat. They both got out and walked nervously up the path to the open front door where Geoff was waiting for them. He just stepped to one side and invited both humans into the house. Poppy was disappointed to be left outside when the door closed, and the garden returned to silence.

In a state of great excitement, Poppy raced back to the shed to wake the others and tell them what she had seen. Oscar wasn't interested, and neither were Romeo and Victor.

"There are always people coming to the house in the morning, Poppy. It's nothing to do with us, so we just ignore it," whispered Oscar.

Trevor and Charlie seemed to feel the same and simply turned away from her. Just as Poppy was about to give up, Flora attracted her attention.

"If no one else is interested, let's you and me go and have a look then, Poppy."

The apathy displayed by Trevor and Charlie annoyed Poppy a little, but it wasn't going to deter her from further investigation. In fact, she was more than happy to be accompanied by Flora on this particular occasion.

With renewed enthusiasm, both young dogs sauntered through the door and walked up to the house. Poppy arrived at the glass door first and looked in, closely followed by Flora. Their reactions to what they saw, however, were completely different. Poppy just peered into the large front room and watched Geoff sitting in his armchair quietly talking to the new couple. Flora, on the other hand, became really agitated, jumping wildly up and down, barking and banging her head against the glass. Geoff heard the ruckus and quickly moved to open the door, which allowed Flora into the room. She was squealing with delight as she leapt into the lady's arms, enthusiastically licking her face.

For a few moments, things became absolutely chaotic. Flora was barking and running about, stopping every so often to nuzzle the faces of both humans. Even though both of the people were crying, Poppy perfectly understood what was happening. Flora had found her human parents. Geoff looked at Poppy, still sitting patiently outside the patio door, and smiled. He liked Poppy a lot and beckoned her inside, so she padded into the house.

At first, Flora didn't even notice the little Lhasa, waiting patiently by the chair but eventually realised Poppy was there and jumped down to face her.

"Poppy. It's my parents, and they've come to take me home! I can't help thinking that, only a few days ago, I was trapped in that horrible van with Trevor and Charlie. I honestly thought that we would never be free again, but you got us out. I owe you everything. You are so clever, and yet I gave you no credit for that at all. I have behaved so badly throughout and nearly let you down. Please forgive me, Poppy."

Geoff was still talking to the humans who followed him, with Flora in tow, out of the house and down to the shed. Only then did Poppy realise that Geoff, thoughtful as ever, was letting Flora say goodbye to her friends. Poppy was so delighted for the little bulldog knowing that she was safely back in the care of her family and would soon be at home where she belonged.

Despite the euphoria engendered by the reunion of Flora with her parents, there was much sadness in the garden that afternoon as she said her goodbyes.

All too soon, following some bittersweet moments, Flora and her parents were gone, and all the dogs felt a little sad.

"Are you okay, Poppy?" Trevor was standing by her side. "You know that Flora is safe now. Be honest, life in the forest never really suited her."

Trevor had been right about that all along because he recognised that Flora could never have endured a life in the wild. Trevor knew what he was talking about. Flora had always been a pampered dog and was completely unsuited to a life of hardship and strife. It made Poppy think about her other friends, particularly the feisty Nina. She wondered how the husky would be coping.

The truth is that Poppy's little group had been incredibly lucky to get this far, and if it hadn't been for Oscar and his friends, they would have all been caught by the villainous humans and inevitably suffered punishment. Thank goodness for Geoff because Poppy now realised that she had no idea how to find her way home.

At that moment, Oscar suggested that they all go down to the beach for a run. The wind was still gusting, but the rain had stopped. Perfect conditions, Poppy thought.

All the dogs wanted to go except Trevor. "I'm still not completely fit, Oscar," he said. "Another time, perhaps." Then, he rolled over with his back to them, settling for rest and recuperation rather than activity.

Once on the beach, all the dogs revelled in their newly found freedom. They were safe and would come to no harm out here in the open. It was wonderful to run and play for a change and not have to worry about all their troubles. It was such a great feeling. After spending most of the afternoon there, all the dogs returned home just as the tide started to come in. Poppy knew how fast that happened but didn't need to worry because Oscar understood the ebb and flow of the sea very well and guided them away in plenty of time.

On returning to Geoff's house, Poppy's Lhasa senses kicked in again with a clear warning of danger. The others had sensed it too and approached the shed with a good deal of caution. This proved to be a very wise move because what they saw next was chilling.

Trevor was face to face with Dima, the huge predator that they had previously encountered on the hillside overlooking the old barn. This ferocious dog had intervened only days ago when a human had seriously injured both Trevor and Billy. Thanks to Dima, the humans had fled.

On that occasion, Poppy had not been this close to him and thus had not appreciated what an awe-inspiring beast he was. The immensely powerful Ovcharka was jet black in colour and as big as Brutus, albeit much heavier in build with powerful jaws. There were now six allies in the shed, including the three German shepherds, but Trevor's assailant dismissed them all with a sneering glance. Poppy looked back at the house, hoping to see Geoff coming down the path, but no luck; he was not there.

Oscar moved forward warily, closely shadowed by Romeo and Victor. The tiny Chihuahua stood still.

Poppy closed in on their adversary and spoke directly to the huge dog. "You helped us before when we needed it, and I believe you helped us last night when you terrified the human who was threatening us. Please walk away now, and you will not be hurt."

Dima was not amused. "Do not try to stop me, little dog. Your threats mean nothing to me. I intend to talk to Milo, and if I don't like what he has to say, then I'll kill him. And if any of you interfere with that, I'll kill you all."

"I won't interfere," Poppy responded bravely, "but I'll not leave either."

"Please go, Poppy," said Trevor, "and take all the others with you. I'll be fine."

Oscar was offended by that. "No, Trevor. We won't go. We are here to support you."

Oscar was sincere and strongly objected to a retreat, even when faced with the massive Ovcharka. The German shepherds were more than capable of defending themselves and would not be told to run. Charlie would not leave either.

Trevor and Dima were still face to face, growling at each other, but neither moved an inch.

Then Trevor spoke. "Everything is under control, Poppy. And so, if none of you will go, please leave everything to me."

Poppy's response was very clear. "None of us will leave, Trevor, and so we'll all be here if you need us."

Dima then turned toward Poppy. "You're a very brave little dog to be standing here facing me. I respect you for it and don't care if you stay. For now, Milo and I have things to discuss."

With that, he turned toward Trevor again and made his meaning very clear with a series of threatening growls.

Poppy was shaking as she responded with a threat but looked Dima in the eye as she did so. "If you kill Trevor, then we will all kill you. There are a lot more of us including a human. Trevor rescued me from captivity and has rescued many others too. He regularly risks his life for other dogs—and you want to kill him? You are nothing but a thug."

"Is that true, Milo?" The Ovcharka emphasised the last word. "You left me to be caught and did nothing, but I see you managed to save yourself. Because of you, I have suffered cruelty beyond your imagination. Nevertheless, I survived because of you. I survived so that one day I could take my revenge on the so-called friend who put his own worthless life before mine.

"I see that you are now calling yourself Trevor. Well, Trevor, my erstwhile defender, you have not been very hard to find. In the wild, animals tell stories about you and your heroic exploits. But what about me? We were allies against the world. What about me, Milo?"

Dima seemed to be visibly upset, and the poignancy of his words moved Poppy.

An emotional Trevor spoke again. "I'm still your friend, Dima. I didn't desert you. I returned to our prison and tried to find you, but you weren't there. I stayed and searched desperately for you every single day for many long months without success. I couldn't leave the forest without you and, as a result, I remained and made my home in the place where you were caught. Other dogs live in the forest with me now and have helped me to liberate many more dogs suffering cruelty at the hands of the same sort of men who were so cruel to you. Stay with me, Dima. Join our group. We all need you."

Dima was quiet now and stepped back away from Trevor. All the dogs present became aware that Dima was conflicted, but it was Poppy who recognised that, having had the opportunity to confront Trevor, Dima's rage had abated, and the hate inside him now burned a little less brightly.

After a short pause, Dima addressed Milo for the final time. "You were always the clever one, Milo. Smarter than me, for sure. I have searched for you endlessly, but I cannot harm you. I don't think I would ever have harmed you. My heart has been full of hate and rage for so many years, and yet here we are, still friends after all. We'll meet again sometime, Milo, but I will not go with you now." Still talking to Trevor, Dima looked directly at Poppy. "You have brave and faithful friends here who are willing to die for you. If only I could say the same."

There were no more words from either dog. Dima rose, raised his head and roared one final time, perhaps to demonstrate his immense power to those present. Seconds later, he strode out of the shed and out of their lives.

Chapter Thirty

Home

Since the climactic face-off between Trevor and the vengeful Dima earlier in the afternoon, Poppy sat alone, trying hard to come to terms with what she had just witnessed. It was remarkable that, even though Dima had decided not to stay, matters between the two dogs had been resolved and a fragile peace established.

After the Ovcharka's abrupt departure, however, Trevor was keen to shut down any further discussion about his past, preferring to concentrate on the more pressing problems of the moment. Nevertheless, in a private conversation with Poppy, he did reveal something of his early life and the cruelty inflicted on both himself and Dima that sparked many painful memories. After confiding in Poppy, Trevor left the general hubbub of the shed and sought peace and tranquillity elsewhere. Although Dima had almost certainly been responsible for saving Trevor's life, his name was not mentioned again.

Sometime later, Geoff arrived back at the house, completely oblivious to the potentially dangerous confrontation that had taken place earlier. Normally, the dogs would be up and about, taking advantage of their much-valued freedom, but there was no sign of any of them, and this gave him cause for concern. Geoff felt that he needed to investigate but, before he was able to do so, a car he did not recognise pulled up outside the front gate. Two people, a man and a woman, got out of the car and approached him to introduce themselves.

Still concerned about the dogs, Geoff ushered the new arrivals into the house and made them comfortable before he returned to the garden to check on his charges. Meanwhile, Trevor had rejoined the others but had not yet engaged in any conversation, preferring to sit alone with his thoughts.

When Geoff reached the shed and looked in on his growing company of dogs, he satisfied himself that all was in order and then invited Poppy up to the house. He didn't ask anyone else, and so she just followed, dawdling behind him, lost in her own thoughts.

"Hurry up, Poppy." Geoff was calling out to her as he opened the front door. "I have a wonderful surprise for you."

As the little dog jumped through the doorway, her incredible senses kicked in, although, on this occasion, the atmosphere was anything but threatening. As she entered the front room and looked up, everything around her seemed to evaporate before her eyes, except for the two people standing there tearfully with open arms.

Poppy could hardly believe what she was seeing because Geoff had found her mum and dad! He had actually done it. Poppy had no idea how and didn't care either, because there they were. She jumped into her mum's arms and kept licking her face, and then did the same thing to her dad.

It seemed an eternity before the little dog calmed down, and even then, it was difficult for her to contain her excitement. For the first five minutes, she raced backwards and forwards, jumped up and down and ran in small circles at speed. Geoff continued talking quietly to her parents until, at last, he invited them all down to the shed.

Once inside, Poppy squeezed herself between Charlie and Trevor, nuzzling them both before settling down. Meanwhile, Geoff was introducing Poppy's parents to all the other dogs one at a time, with Trevor left until last.

"This dog is quite a remarkable animal," Geoff said quietly. "He seems to have the ability not only to bond with other dogs but to control them, quickly and easily. When I first encountered him, he had been seriously injured twice, once as the result of an electrical burn and then by a significant blow to the head. Regardless of the pain he must have been experiencing, he still managed to gain the confidence of my own dogs to the extent that all three, former police dogs at that, defied me for the first time ever. This Patterdale, I'm sorry, but I don't know his name, did all that in a matter of hours. The fact is that he is highly intelligent and able to communicate his wishes to humans and dogs alike.

"Poppy is very similar in many ways and showed her own significant leadership abilities by taking control of the group when the Patterdale passed out as a result of the injuries he sustained. The two of them make an impressive team. The Chihuahua also has no name that I know of but has lived a feral life for years, according to my vet. I know you may think me a little foolish, but I believe these dogs were actually looking for you. Don't ask me why I think that, because I won't be able to tell you. The thing is that they had numerous opportunities to leave my care but chose not to, and I simply have no idea why."

While Geoff was speaking, Poppy was telling all her friends that she was going home. Her dad was speaking.

"What are you going to do about the Patterdale and the Chihuahua, Mr Brown?"

Geoff looked pensive and then replied. "I don't know Mr James. I really don't. I'll probably just let them go. Neither dog will ever be tamed, and I have three dogs already. To be honest, that's more than enough for me."

"We'll take them," Mrs James said firmly. "It seems that Poppy has an obvious bond with them, and that's good enough for me."

"Are you sure, Mrs James?" Geoff seemed surprised. "They might prove to be a handful."

"We're sure." Poppy's mum replied in a tone that brooked no argument.

"Okay then!" replied Geoff. "In that case, I need to explain one or two things to you before you go."

The conversation only lasted a short while, and Poppy's parents seemed happy with what Geoff had told them. That was it, really. A done deal! One minute Poppy was expecting to part company with her friends, and the next, they were both travelling home with her.

Poppy knew that Trevor needed time to fully recuperate and, if she had anything to do with it, that was exactly what he was going to get. Charlie, on the other hand, just needed a home.

When at last, after a long journey, they arrived at Poppy's family home, Mr James introduced Trevor and Charlie to their new surroundings. Poppy was very impatient to show them around but had to wait for her dad to take them. There was no way that he was going to lose Poppy again. Trevor looked around at what he considered to be his temporary home and breathed a sigh of relief. Here he would be safe. Here he could regain his strength and, when the time was right, begin the long journey home.

Of course, Trevor and Charlie refused to sleep in the house, understandably preferring to bed down in the small barn adjacent to the house, but this was not a problem. In a brief conversation earlier, Geoff had detailed Trevor's discernible requirement that he be free to go or stay as he pleased. Poppy's parents had listened carefully and were quite happy to go along with it, at least temporarily. This meant that, regardless of the weather conditions, the barn door would always remain open.

As in all things connected with Trevor, his recovery was remarkable and, after only a few weeks, he felt ready and able to leave. And so, on a chilly November morning, he called both Charlie and Poppy to a meeting in the garden where he informed them that it was time for him to begin the journey home.

"I don't know exactly when, Poppy, but it will be soon."

Charlie looked utterly crestfallen and pressed Trevor to stay longer. "The thing is, Trevor, I absolutely love it here and would really like to stay. I'm not confident about any of this. I mean, I'm really unsure. You and I have been together for so long that I don't know how I'll cope without you. On the other hand, I've never had a forever home before, and to me, this feels like it. All my life, I've suffered cruelty, right up to the moment I met you, Trevor. I will never ever be disloyal to you, so if you want me to go back with you, then I will. What else can I do?"

"Charlie, you've been such a wonderful friend to me," Trevor replied sadly, "and I'll miss you more than you know — but I think you've earned the right to make your own choice about your future. I'll miss you too, Poppy, but you both have to understand that I can't stay. I must go back. Remember, I left seven dogs behind when I embarked on this journey, including Billy. Now I need to know if they are safe and still free. I cannot forget that the men running the compound are still in business, so there is much to do."

Trevor was quiet for a while, and he looked wistfully at his companions. His emotions were clear when he continued. "For now, though, let's just enjoy the moment."

Trevor stayed for longer than Poppy thought he would, happy to sleep on his own in her dad's barn. One morning, however, as the first frost appeared on the grass, Poppy ran out to the barn to see him, but the empty structure told its own story. Trevor had gone and, even though both little dogs were sad, they accepted that Trevor had responsibilities to more than just the two of them.

Over the following weeks, Poppy often wondered where he was and whether he had been reunited with his friends back in the forest. She wondered how they all were and, of course, she thought about Charmaine, that extraordinary cat and what adventures she might be having. Sadly, that adventure now had to be left behind because Poppy was home, safe and sound, and that was where she was determined to stay.

Printed in Great Britain
by Amazon

76790426R00156